# MIDAS

Peter Birkett Thompson

*For my mum Maureen & my sister Denise.*

*Please visit :*

*https://www.facebook.com/Peter-Birkett-Author-100132942611715*

*and:*

*https://www.amazon.co.uk/Peter-Birkett/e/B09JP3QSH8/ref=aufs_dp_fta_dsk*

*For newsletter, bio and info on other titles and upcoming releases. Kindest regards!*

# 1

Father Jones had been put on standby; he may have been needed, at *The Haven*, to give Jason Steadman his last rites, probably sooner rather than later. He was expecting a call from Jason's family at any moment. The Haven was described by its owner as an *alternativ*e medical facility. Some might have described it as a last chance saloon, although it's owner would never have talked of it in such crass terms.

Jason lay in one of the Haven's beds in a private room. His eyes were closed through exhaustion. His family had left for a while after being there at his side for most of the day. Jason hadn't opened his eyes, moved or uttered a word for hours. He had cancer and had been told that it was inoperable. He'd had a second opinion and neither one had given him much hope; just weeks rather than months and to forget about seeing Christmas.

In desperation and with nothing else to lose, Jason's family had moved him into this facility that used ground breaking, effective, alternative methods of healing...or so the owner had told them two days previously. His family had put their remaining, dwindling, faith in the patented machines and new treatments that were starting to cause a murmur in the medical world.

The sound of faint footsteps grew slightly louder amid the background hum and whirr of the Haven's unique equipment, until the outline of a figure appeared at the entrance to Jason's room. John, the cleaner, scanned the room and checked that the patient was alone. Jason's personal belongings were on the table next to his bed. Slowly, John stepped forward. He looked intently at the patient. From his right hand, he removed a blue latex glove and then he rested his palm briefly on the forehead of the patient. Several seconds passed as the machines still hummed and bleeped, then, Mr Steadman's eyes slowly opened.

◆ ◆ ◆

In a modest sized flat, Andrew Gold woke up next to an empty space. On waking, sometimes he forgot for a split second about the last few month's events and then he saw the empty space next to him and remembered. He got out of bed, wrapped around a dressing gown and sleepily drew open the bedroom curtains, before leaving to an adjacent bedroom where his seven year old son, Jack, was still asleep.

"Hey, you awake yet Jack? It's time to get up." Andy was made to jump by his energetic and early rising four year old daughter Fran, who ran into his legs and wrapped her arms around him.

"Hi, good morning!" he scooped up his daughter, carried her downstairs and sat her down on the sofa.

"Would you like to watch some cartoons before school?" he asked. Fran nodded enthusiastically. Andy flicked on the tv and selected the cartoon channel before going to the kitchen, where he was joined by Jack. Andy went over to him and gently adjusted his collar and jumper.

None of these three were used to this situation or were happy with it, but the kids seemed to have adapted quickly. The split from his wife was still a non-healed wound to Andy though. They had seemed to be the *golden* family; all fair haired, including his estranged wife, although hers came from a bottle.

"What do you want for breakfast Jack?" Andy asked.

"Cereal please dad."

"Apple juice?" Jack nodded. Andy filled a small glass from the fridge and handed it to him. He filled another and placed it in Jack's other hand, "Give this one to your sister."

"What if she wants orange dad?"

"If you're having apple, she'll want the same." Andy smiled and Jack headed off to the sitting room, not really understanding his dad's preferred drink logic, but sure enough, Fran was quite happy with the apple juice. Andy poured a mug of coffee that had been brewing and made a face like he'd just taken a hit from a drug. Cup in hand he returned to the living room, "I know we should be sat at the table but we're running a bit late so you can watch tv. Do you want some cereal Fran?" Fran gave up one second of cartoon time to look up at Andy.

"Yes please dad, the small boxes. It's my turn to pick first."

"It doesn't matter today because it's a new packet and there are two of each kind." Andy said. Fran took her eyes off the tv and studied the boxes of different cereals carefully, looking at each one intently.

"Which one are you having?" she asked Jack.

"Krispies." replied Jack.

"I'll have sugar puffs." Fran decided.

"Dad, why does Fran always have the same drink as me, but never the same cereal?" enquired Jack, quietly. Andy smiled and shrugged.

"I don't know pal, it's one of life's mysteries." Fran was oblivious as she watched tv and ate. Jack shrugged. Andy was worried about the effect the split has had on Jack more than Fran, who just seemed to have taken it in her stride, but the difference in years had made it more difficult for Jack. He always said he was fine when asked, but had seemed melancholy and troubled for the last few months. All Andy could do was keep an eye on him.

◆ ◆ ◆

Half an hour later, Andy's twelve year old Ford pulled up outside the school. He lifted Fran out of her car seat and then they followed Jack up to the playground.

"When do I get to come to this school Dad?" Fran asked: she was in the reception class in a nearby building.

"Not long now; are you looking forward to it?" Fran nodded with her usual enthusiasm.

"But...I don't want to leave my own school."

"Oh, ok, I'm not sure whether that's possible."

"I will ask Miss Perkins." Fran said. She supposed that Miss Perkins, her teacher, could reconcile anything. Andy called to Jack about his lunch box that he'd forgotten and Fran zipped over to give it to him.

"Your Mum will pick you up Jack. I'll see you next week." Jack held his hand up to signify that he understood. Then Andy walked with Fran to the next building which was her reception class. She stood by him holding his hand until some other children came into the playground and then she looked up at Andy as if to say *gotta go.* A teacher was overseeing them so Andy shouted to Fran that he was leaving.

"See you later. Have a good day." he said.

Andy got to the car and then glanced back to the school. The tinge of sadness at leaving them for another five days was not something that he was getting used to.

# 2

Andy was now switching back to work mode. If you had asked him at school, as the careers officer did, what he wanted to be when he left, the last thing he would have replied would have been "a *Chef*." Well, perhaps it wouldn't have been the last thing, but it would have been fairly low on the list, perhaps just above "*hairdresser*". He sometimes wondered how and why he happened to take that path. When at college studying "A" level subjects, he used to make jokes about the catering students because they all seemed a bit... well... dumb. Perhaps karma had paid him back for the quips he used to make, by putting him in that world.

Needing a job desperately, he'd taken one as a kitchen porter, which turned out to be a fancy name for a pot-washer, in a large hotel. From the sink, he'd observed with some jealousy, the chefs in their white jackets, the ones creating all the different sized pans that needed scrubbing. They were higher up the hotel pecking order and seemed to command a level of respect; they could get angry and everybody was ok with that. What they did seemed exciting and so he began watching what they did and then started to ask if he could help. The chefs soon tired of his questions and enthusiasm: as *kitchen porter,* he was viewed in the same manner Romans did with their slaves. He'd also asked the Hotel manager, who had made it widely known at any and every oppurtunity that *he* had started off at the very bottom of the ladder scrubbing pans, if he could become a trainee chef at the same hotel... but he said *no*. The manager obviously had not been inspired to give anyone else the chance of improvement that he himself had been offered. He was needed in the trenches. So, undettered and determined to wear that white jacket, he talked his way into a trainee chef job somewhere else and went on from there. The first two or three years *were* exciting, after that work became a bit of a chore and it was a *lot* harder than it had seemed from the sink. What he *should* have asked the chefs back in the hotel was...*what's it like, do you still enjoy it?* The tv shows that made the life of a chef appear exciting and/or glamorous quickly seemed a con. The other thing was, it didn't pay great, though it *was* more than minimum rate and he felt that he was tied to it for the foreseeable future.

Eventually the old Ford arrived at his current

place of work, *The Eagle*, a pub/restaurant. The place hadn't seen a coat of paint in a while and had a *sale/lease* sign sticking out like a sore thumb. He parked up and got out. Ringing the side doorbell got no response, so he made his way to a window that looked in to the bar area, where he spotted Gaz, the barman, talking to the cleaner. Andy gestured through the window. Gaz got up off his stool and trundled off to open the side door.

"Alright Andy?" Gaz asked.

"It's ok, I'll just freeze out there."

"Sorry mate, I was just talking." Gaz said. *Aren't you always.* "Anyway, the doorbell isn't working."

"Then you and the doorbell have a lot in common." said Andy. Gaz was slightly bemused by that comment but grinned non-the-less as Andy walked past him.

"Busy last night was it?" Andy asked.

"Not really, Mark was wasted by eight...and the Jack Daniels bottle is almost empty. It was changed in the morning." Gaz continued with some more details about some customers from the previous night who had complained, Andy displayed a genuine lack of interest as he headed towards the kitchen. Mark, the manager, was well known to be overly fond of Jack Daniels.

"Yeah tell me later pal, I have got to switch the equipment on." Andy added as a parting gift to Gaz, who continued telling the story to the cleaner as though she was originally his intended audience.

Another member of the kitchen team, Mick, joined Andy. Mick was a good guy. Plenty of people in catering were not. Perhaps they all felt that they had been duped as Andy did. Andy had met some decent people over the years and Mick was solidly in that relatively small group. Mick was quite thin, a year older than Andy, at thirty three, and he liked to say that made him a little bit wiser. Andy had a theory that you could tell if a workmate was decent or not by whether they would cover a shift for you if you needed them to, or if they couldn't, whether or not they looked genuinely sorry that they couldn't. Mick would cover a shift if needed.

"Good days off?" Mick asked.

"Not too bad." Andy noticed a minor flood in the kitchen, "I see the dishwasher pipes are leaking again. About time they called a plumber out, I'm getting sick of this."

"More chance of Mark calling in *Ghostbusters* than a plumber." Mick said, "They cost money. And anyway, there are only two people that he's interested in and that's *Jack* and *Daniels*. Look on the bright side, at least tommorrow you can bring in a rubber duck."

"Rubber duck?"

A waitress, Nadia, entered the kitchen. She

was in her mid thirties and quite chirpy. She exercised daily, almost obsessively.

"Hi lads." she greeted.

"I'm so glad it's you in today. That warm greeting and beaming smile." Mick replied.

"Yeah…sure." Flattery stopped working on Nadia about a decade previously.

"Honestly...plus you make the best coffee I've ever tasted." Mick added.

"It comes from a machine. All I do is press a button."

"Yeah, but it's the way you press the button; you got the magic touch. Go on do it again for me."

"Why not just say *Nadia, would you get me a coffee?* You know you're the reason we get two cases of coffee delivered every week, before you came it was only one." Nadia rolled her eyes.

"Do you think Mark has noticed?" Mick wondered.

"Not a chance of that. I'm only amazed you can sleep at night."

"I'm kept awake thinking about you."

Gaz approached the grill area. In his hand he had his mobile phone and he was grinning, once again, waiting or hoping to see if anyone asked him about the message he had received. Andy noticed this and deliberately continued with his work until Gaz had been standing there for some time. Eventually, just to get rid of him, Andy asked.

"Got an important message there Gaz? Is it from the Prime Minister?" Gaz grinned again but still said nothing.

"Is it from a...*girl*?" Mick asked.

"It's not the PM, it's Karen." replied Gaz, before walking back to the bar area. Not that Andy or Mick could care less who it was from.

"Gaz has a new friend. Keeps him quiet." Mick commented, "Which can't be a bad thing. Although this *coy* act he puts on when he gets a text message is a bit baffling. That guy would talk all day, nonstop, if we actually looked like we were listening to him." surmised Mick.

"Amen to that." Andy said. After less than one hour in Mick's company he felt lighter...not as burdened. He appreciated and noticed the effect people have on each other a lot more clearly in these past few months.

"Bet he talks in his sleep." said Mick.

"Maybe we should ask Karen? On second thoughts, probably best to just nod and walk past, like I did this morning."

"Imagine if we actually *did* take in the crap he comes out with, one conversation would run into another; it would be like being stuck in Groundhog Day. Our lives would cease to hold any meaning."

"Well the only meaning your life has at the moment is *getting the beers in* and *which waitress is working*." joked Andy. Gaz reappeared; for once his facial expression suggested that he may have something relevant or meaningful to say.

"Oh by the way, I forgot to mention. This place has been sold. All the staff have been given two weeks notice." he stated, before sauntering off again.

# 3

In his office Dom was feeling smug. It was a jacket of smugness that he wore on a daily basis. He was about to make the call to Jason Steadman's wife to tell her the good news. He'd made this type of call on several previous occasions and every time it felt like he'd gotten away with something and received a large slice of fortune that he didn't deserve. The responses to the good news always gave him the *energy* that he craved; energy he could only get from other people. Attention, adulation or indeed *any* kind of response was fuel to him and needed fuel to fill a void that he felt inside. It didn't have to be positive energy or responses, negative energy would do just as well, as long as it was a reaction of *some* kind, it would regulate his emotions. He knew about all this on some level, but very rarely did this knowledge make it into his consciousness, and if it did, it was rapidly dismissed to the back burner. To the back burner of a stove that he didn't own.

Sure enough, the gushing emotional response

coming through the speaker was music to Dom's ears and extra validation that topped up his reservoir. He explained to her, once again, how the ground breaking machines were changing what could be achieved medically. The lady on the other end of the call had heard him say the words *"significant recovery"*. She almost didn't believe it. She was going to have to see it to believe it and was already en-route to the Haven when she had received the call.

Thirty minutes later, she arrived, along with her daughter Stephanie and her daughter's sceptical husband, Stephen, who had thought this whole escapade was a complete waste of time *and* money; although a fee had never been set in stone; it had seemed wrong to agree a concrete fee and neither party had discussed it. Dom had noticed the expensive Mercedes they had left parked on the car park and he floated the idea that it was a *no win no fee* type of deal. Stephen had thought it wrong to give people false hope, and that this Dominic character was some kind of *quack*. Some, quite substantial, part of him didn't wish to be proved wrong.

Walking quickly through the immaculate corridors, they passed John, who was steadily polishing the floor outside Jason's room. Dom was waiting for them at Jason's door, his shadow overlapping John's on the corridor floor. He urged them to be quiet as Jason was still quite weak.

When Mrs Steadman opened the door, she saw her husband sitting up in the bed, breathing, it appeared, quite normally. He was drinking a cup of tea and he offered a spontaneous smile at the entrance of the three of them.

"My God." was the initial response from Mrs Steadman. She went over to Jason's side and gently embraced him, "It's Incredible."

Moved to the side of the room was the apparatus that the Haven had been using to heal Jason. It looked similar to other more conventional machines, from the outside at least, what was on the inside was a mystery...some kind of magic judging by the transformation of the patient. On the side of the machines was the logo of *Pearce Industries.*

"We are giving him a break from treatment for a few hours. But he will receive more until we are satisfied the process is complete." Dom said.

"Wonderful! Absolutely amazing! Thankyou so....*so* much." Stephanie gushed emotion. Dom smiled in response and in his mind he set an *applicable* fee.

◆ ◆ ◆

These machines, the ones that Dom professed cured all ailments, were developed and built as a bit of a gimmick. Originally, when Dom had set up the Haven, he had done so because he wanted to help people and create something unique...or at least that's what he had told people at the time it was being converted from an old mill.

Dom had been left a lot of money when his father died; something in the low millions, and he had invested it wisely in the right property at the right time. It didn't take a genius to buy up auctioned or disused buildings and renovate them...it just took funds, which he'd been handed on a platter. It *did* take a methodical approach and consistency and also some patience. He was now personally worth, in property and money in the bank, over five times what he started out with ten years ago.

Making money, the thing that had held his undivided attention back in the day, now offered less excitement and appeal. He had become bored with the property business and so now employed someone, on exactly the going rate, to run that side of things for him.

He had originally conceived the Haven whilst slightly drunk at a dinner party. One of the other guests had described it at the time as just a *vanity project*, after he had left the room. Alhough Dom was not aware of this on a conscious level, this was true....it was the *epitome* of a vanity project, or *fuel supply generator*. He would be the focal point of this project with all the attention and fuel his grandiose self needed, and then some.

Now that it had been constructed and his

after dinner dream had become a reality, he strode the halls of his facility like a modern day guru and, in his own warped way of thinking... the star of his own movie. Here he had all the confirmation he needed that he was *indeed* something special. Concrete proof that his father had been incorrect when labelling him as *useless*, back in his formative years. *Nothing he ever did was good enough?* Well he was now proving that wrong emphatically. Of course, this sentiment simmered underneath Dom's conscious state, somewhere on that stove that he didn't own.

◆ ◆ ◆

The Haven's machines were the product of collaboration between Dom himself and Sven Kuber. Sven was a well talked about figure in the world of self-healing and somewhat of an authority on the un-tapped potential of the human brain. Although, unless you were into these types of subjects, you would most likely never have heard of him. He had once featured on the *TV Norge* news channel in a special report. He had stayed for 24 hours in a lake of ice and he had also, on another occasion, climbed Norway's Glittertind Mountain in just his underpants. He chose the Calvin Kline brand and presumably had some sort of sponsership deal. His secret to achieving these seemingly impossible tasks remained a mystery, unless you were willing to pay and to also sign a non disclosure agreement, keeping the secrets, secret. But he did say, in whatever form of advertising he used, that the secret to unlocking this hidden within all of us potential, hinged on special breathing techniques and the use of naturally occurring but rare crystals.

These two main principles: energy passing through crystals, and a prototype ventilator/ breathing apparatus, were the core of the Haven's alternative healing techniques. There were also the faith healing sessions performed by Dom himself and a select few others.

Originally, Dom had contacted Sven, along with faith healers, psychics and other similarly alternative individuals, because that was the sort of vibe he was aiming for at the Haven. He had heard, at that dinner party, one of the other guests *vanity project* comment and wanted to show them, let them know how serious he was. But to him, really, it was all a source of entertainment and he found it a buzz attracting all the rich and, as he saw it, *gullible* and/or *desperate* members of the public that might fall for the subject matter on offer. Many of these rich, and often fairly soulless people, actually thought that they could *buy into* spiritualism. *Everything had a price*. Others had lost faith in or had run out of options using conventional medicine and were willing to try anything. There was money involved; these people had money burning holes in their designer suits and Gucci handbags.

Dom did state that it was to be a non-profit organization... officially. The property trade had levelled out. It still made him money, but there was zero fun in that process anymore. Back when he was making ridiculous profits *that* was fun. Money made from the Haven, the lottery funding and donations, gave him more satisfaction because it felt like ill-gotten-gains and the best part was, he could use the Haven to his advantage for tax purposes. Dom felt his best when he was winning on every possible level.

Dom had commissioned these healing machines, which had been copyrighted and then built by two separate manufacturers, so neither knew exactly what was going on, and they were *off-set* against other income at an inflated rate. Did he actually think that any of them worked? Not really...although he didn't dismiss the usefulness of the acupuncture practitioner; even if she was freelance and just renting out a room there. So, the Haven was a multi faceted project. He saw himself as a magician; he needed more than just pulling a rabbit out of a hat in order to have a good act.

When people actually started to be cured, that surprised him, and at first he thought it was just pure coincidence. Extremely good publicity, but, none-the-less coincidence. Then the cures started happening too regularly to be considered mere chance. *Could there be more to these machines? Some genuine substance?* Was Sven actually a genius, and not just a man in his underpants wandering around in the snow? Sven himself did not seem surprised with the successful results.

"Of course. The crystals return the body's cells to their original and natural state." he had said.

The miraculous cures had begun happening all at once and after some time you could stop counting them on your fingers and word really started to spread. The Haven was a little ripple in a pond at first, then a bigger stone had been thrown in creating bigger, further reaching waves.

To Dom, this was a double edged sword. His grandiose self liked to think he knew everything, that he was always one step ahead of everyone else, but, these machines actually curing cancer? It didn't compute in his lizard-like brain. There was something that he was missing. Was he going to have to bite the bullet and recognise that these machines were actually genuine? Genuine was a concept that didn't sit easily with him, in whatever the circumstance, whether it be genuine friendship, a genuine business deal or whatever. In fact, *genuine* in any form felt like an alien concept to him and as such, slightly unsettling.

◆ ◆ ◆

The first of the *actual* healings had taken place on the fifteenth of March; a meaningless date to Dom, until it cropped up once again, by mere chance, during the annual staff reviews with Penny, the facility's general manager. To be more specific, the review was for a member of staff who went by the name of *Johnathon Colin Marshall...D.O.B...23/07/1958... Cleaner...Startdate...**15/03**.*

That's when Dom's ears pricked up. Normally he would have delegated this tedious task, but he cross-referenced all of the incidents of the *miraculous* recoveries with all the times that John had been on duty. There was a direct link. *How Bizarre.* John was on duty on *every* occasion. Then Dom went a level deeper and checked CCTV footage from within the facility. It took a lot of time and effort and, again, he wished he could have delegated the task, but there it was on the screen. The cleaner, John, had come into physical contact with each recovered patient. Dom had painstakingly slowed down each peice of footage and had noted John placing his hand upon each patient. As bizarre and amazing as it seemed, this run of the mill cleaner appeared to have some *actual* healing powers. Dom didn't really understand how this was possible, but he had figured it out himself. *Always one step ahead.* If this was true and this employee had the power to heal, then Dom wouldn't rock the boat. It took him very little time to accept the sheer wonder of the situation, and the fact that the thing that he had been pretending to do actually existed and was being practiced by someone else. He assimilated all of this and then decided he would manipulate the situation to his own advantage… as per usual.

# 4

Andy had picked the kids up on his next day off, and he, Jack and Fran were shopping in the local supermarket. Fran was putting various things that were within reach into the trolley. Then Jack held them up to Andy who gave either a nod or a shake of the head to signal to Jack whether to put the things back on the shelf or keep them in the trolley. It was a workable system they had developed. Out of the blue, whilst replacing a box of *slimming crackers*, Jack asked.

"Dad, are you ever going to come back?"

"Well your mum.....I would if I could."

"Why can't you? Does she not like you anymore?"

"I wish I could say...I'm not really sure." Andy tried to say it as lightly as possible.

"My friend at school, Zach, his dad doesn't live at his house anymore."

"Lots of dad's don't dude. But it's never the kids fault. Just grown-ups messing things up."

"Did you mess things up? Mum said you did."

Jack asked.

Andy did his best to bite his lip and not apportion any blame. “Sometimes mums and dads fall out. Sometimes they make friends again…sometimes they don’t.”

“Is that what you and mum have done, fallen out?"

“I think so.”

Fran came back to the trolley with her arms full of snacks.

“Dad, I’ll need six of these.”

“Oh, why six?” Andy asked.

“Monday, Tuesday, Thursday, Friday.”

“What about Wednesday?” Jack said.

“Oh yes, Wednesday. Why did I forget about Wednesday. I’ll need another.”

“You only need five Fran. It’s five days.” Jack corrected.

“Alright show-off.” Fran said, before marching back to the shelf to put one back, then she went in search for some other items to add to the ever expanding shopping trolley contents. Andy resumed his conversation with Jack.

“So anyway, about coming back, we’ll have to see how it goes. I'll still see you two as much as possible. You’ll hardly know I’m not at home.”

“Ok. I wish mum would stop being silly though.” Jack said.

Andy smiled at him, and then ruffled his hair. “It’ll be all right.”

A woman shopper recognized Andy, came walking over, and started making a fuss of the children: it was Molly, a neighbour of Jane's mother.

"Has she sent you out shopping? Mum's probably having a bit of peace and quiet eh, while you're all out." Molly said. Andy smiled awkwardly. Fran answered.

"Dad doesn't know what mum is doing."

"What lovey?" enquired Molly.

"Dad doesn't know...he's not speaking to mum..*at the moment*." Jack said. Molly looked a little embarrassed.

"Oh...well, don't wear your dad out. See you later!" With that Molly bustled on her way.

"She's annoying." Jack stated. Andy agreed.

"She is pal."

After they had finished shopping, Andy and the children were emptying the contents of the trolley into the back of his car.

"Do we have to go home now?" Jack asked.

"Well, I have to work later I'm afraid."

"Don't be afraid dad." chirped Fran.

"It's ok Fran; I didn't mean I actually *am* afraid."

"Can't we come with you?" Jack asked.

"I'll be cooking stuff."

"What kind of stuff?" Fran asked.

"Chicken and things like that. I'd love you guys to come, but you wouldn't be able to help."

"We could hold the plates for you." offered Jack.

Andy started to fill up with emotion, but tried not to let the children see it.

"Plates can get hot you know guys, you have to be careful. Maybe when you get a bit older you can help then."

◆ ◆ ◆

He hadn't yet got used to dropping the kids off at his old house; not in the weeks since the split. It was still as traumatic every time. It had seemed that there was little chance of reconciliation, yet the chance was still there, however remote, *until* this new guy showed up on the radar. She had described him as just a friend. Mick had said, *"Don't they always?"* Anyway, as yet nothing was certain. Perhaps Jane would snap out of this spell she was under just as quickly as she had gone under it. Once again though, he was greeted with an ice cold reception. "*Hard-faced*" his father had called her...along with some other choice phrases.

They had met at work, when they were both nineteen. She had pursued *him* and, without any really good reason not to, he had gone with it. They were what many people described as, *a likeable couple*. Their relationship wasn't perfect, but then whose was? She was like a different person now though. Was it his fault for making accusations of infidelity? Did she take it that badly that whatever feelings she had for him were banished to Siberia? That would explain the *ice cold* reception. The punishment didn't seem to fit the crime.

The house was rented and in her name, though he had never imagined that would ever become an issue. Andy had actually still paid towards the rent after moving out but now that had stopped. Jane came out of the door with something to say. She looked at a spot around Andy's left ear, and then cleared her throat.

"There's a *slight* possibility we might be moving." She just dropped that bomb out of the blue…no warning shots. Andy glimpsed a man's shadow in the house behind her.

"Moving?" he asked.

"There is actually *more* than a slight possibility." she repeated. He hadn't misheard. He looked up at the clear blue sky, not a cloud in it.

"Where to?" he asked.

"Look, you know about Rick. I wish *you* could meet someone and move on."

"Rick, you mean the *just good friend* Rick? Where to?"

"It's only 200 miles away."

"200?! Only? Why go so far?"

"You'll still get to see the kids."

"200 miles, no, that's too far."

"It's not definite yet."

"Then why mention it unless it is. Is this something to do with him?" Andy gestured to the house. He thought he could see Rick in the shadows, with a smirk on his face.

"Rick you mean?"

"Who else would I be talking about? Unless you have someone else on the go as well?"

"Now you are being childish."

"Am I? You telling me that guy was just a friend was being childish. Why didn't you just come clean?"

"We did start out just as friends."

"What, for five minutes?"

"Look, this isn't getting us anywhere, I'm going in." With that, she turned and went back into the house. The kids had gone to the window and were waving to their dad as he got back into the car and drove away.

# 5

Later, Andy arrived at work for the evening shift. His mind was darting back and forth trying to make sense of the last hour. He got changed into his uniform under a darker cloud, before moving to the main kitchen where Mick was whistling whilst he put away supplies.

"Buenos dias amigo." Mick greeted.

"Hi man."

Mick noticed that Andy looked more troubled than he had earlier. "Que pasa?" Mick asked. Andy shrugged as he began helping with the delivery.

"Why the Spanish?"

"I was going for Mexican."

"You mean Spanish."

"No, Mexican." Mick affirmed.

"Mexicans speak Spanish don't they? You know, the Spanish went over to South America a few hundred years ago. *The Conquistadors*." added Andy.

"The who? You mean the ones that robbed all their gold, they taught them how to speak

Spanish?"

"Something like that."

"That was good of them. What's *Gringo* then, Spanish or Mexican?"

"Aww...God knows. Were you watching cowboy films this afternoon by any chance?"

"How did you know that?"

"Just a wild guess."

"Awesome guess. Anyway, why the long face?"

"It's Jane, she's talking about moving."

"Moving? Where to?"

"She didn't say, only that it was 200 miles away."

"She may just be winding you up. She probably won't."

"I don't know Mick; she says I need to move on. I don't know what to expect from her anymore. That guy was in the house."

"*Mr wonderful?* Man, that is harsh." Mick surmised. They continued putting the order away for a minute or two whilst Mick thought of the best thing to say, "Maybe you should go on a date. If that's it with Jane, maybe you do need to move on. Unless you can see you two getting back together?"

"Not now." Andy shook his head.

"Then I've got the perfect girl for you."

"No, man."

"What have you got to lose? Well, she's 27, I think, and she thinks you're cute. She's seen you in passing."

"She's not married is she?"

"No, don't be daft."

"Hmm, I don't know."

"Man, it's been months since you split with Jane now. You should start dating again, it would do you good."

"Suppose you *might* have a point."

The two spent a short time doing separate jobs and preparing the kitchen for service time. Andy hadn't been on a date for ten years. Then he made a decision.

"Ok. I'll do it."

"Great. Here's her number." Andy took a scrumpled piece of paper off Mick, "When are you going to call her?" Mick asked, holding a cauliflower in each hand.

"Later."

"Later. I know you...you won't."

"I will. Later."

"Call her now and then it's done with."

"Maybe I'll send her a text." Andy suggested.

"No call her. Text's are too weak of an introduction."

"She might be busy now."

"Come on man, just ring and ask her if she wants to go for a drink. What do you have to lose?"

Andy shrugged and, partly against his better judgement, he decided to go along with Mick's advice. He moved to the back door and called the number. A minute or two later, he came back into the kitchen.

"Well?" Mick enquired.

"Yeah, I'm meeting her next week for a drink."

"Good stuff. This will do you good. Some female company and...whatever else happens."

"Ok dude, but if she looks like a Ukrainian weight-lifter, or is pregnant or something like that, I will never , *ever,* listen to you again."

"Pal, trust your old friend. I'm wise like Yoda. It will at least take your mind off the other crap."

"Well Yoda is a Muppet remember so you do have something in common."

"True...oh before I forget, there's a job I found for you."

"A job, where?" Andy asked.

"It's a place called *the Haven,* they have a café and guess what, it's *nine to five*."

"That would be a lot better. Have you applied?" Andy asked.

"Not my scene really; I have a couple of other irons in the fire. What do you think?"

"Sounds alright."

"I'm glad you said that because you have an interview there on Friday."

"You booked me an interview?"

"Yeah, I thought you could always cancel if you didn't fancy it."

"What are you now...my fairy godmother?"

"Ha ha, things are looking up for you, big changes are coming." Mick said, as he attempted to juggle with three tomatoes.

"Let's hope so." Andy added, as he looked down at the floor at the squashed red fruit.

"Si Signor."

◆ ◆ ◆

That night Andy felt unsettled. He tried watching tv, but kept getting up and doing something else. He looked around the flat; there were no pictures on the walls, or any other visible signs that he had personalised it. Not doing so might make his current situation less real. He might wake up one day, move this stuff out and move back *home*. Was *this* really his home now?

The future seemed quite bleak. There was something at the back of his mind, something happening in the not too distant future, but he had no idea what it could be. He couldn't sense whether it was going to be positive or negative. Perhaps it was the new job or even the girl from the date turning out to be the girl of his dreams. *Like it or not, Jane was now off the menu, out of stock, gone off, past use by date,* or been placed into *deep freeze.* Whichever way he imagined it didn't make it any easier. Perhaps he'd find some pictures for the bare walls in the charity shop... funds were very tight still. He'd get one per week.

Maybe a bath mat and a rug. Maybe it would start to feel like home little by little.

As he was wandering, he saw a faint light in the distance. It was dark and murky all around, except for that light and the two other patches of light near to him. He wondered what that other light might be as it got a little nearer. He looked down. He'd wandered right to the edge of a cliff, *was it Dover?* It was hard to tell where he was. There was no sea or English channel. The other light got nearer. The two other lights stayed by his side. *Was there a face in the light?* He took another step and teetered on the edge. Before he fell off into oblivion, the light seemed to reach out to him. Then he woke. A look at his phone told him it was 4:00 am. He walked to the window and looked out. It was misty and the almost full moon shone down brightly. It was the only bright light out there.

# 6

Friday came around quickly. Andy found the Haven fairly easily, although if you weren't actually looking for it you wouldn't know it was there. It was a turn off from the main road that changed into a track that looked like it led nowhere, that suddenly became tarmac again.

Through a canopy of old sycamore trees, a large white building appeared unexpectedly, it was immaculate and impressive. Dark green leafy shrubs lined the peaceful looking path from the car park to the front entrance. He parked on the car park that was filled with expensive looking, Jaguar's and German pedigree vehicles, plus one white Range Rover deluxe with a personalized number plate ending in *DP*.

Andy'd had so many interviews that he no longer got nervous before-hand. He was usually so relaxed, it was almost as if he didn't really want the job. He didn't. Someone once commented how impressed they were that he was able to get jobs very easily, but the reality was that people weren't exactly queuing up for jobs in catering. It was generally badly paid and the hours were relentless. It looked exciting on the countless tv shows, but many people joining the trade often became disenchanted, as Andy had, within a few years. Unless you won the catering lottery and became a celebrity chef, it was a dire and thankless trade to go into. On a more positive note, it meant that there was little competition for jobs. This, though, was a 9-5...a rarity, the *Holy Grail.*

He fixed his shirt before leaving his car and headed towards the entrance. He glanced back at his old Ford; the poor thing looked a little out of place sat in the middle of the BMW's and Audi's, like an unwelcome gate-crasher to the Oscars.

A heavy glass door led through to the reception. The walls inside were also painted pure white and just as immaculate looking as the outside. The marble floor was highly polished; so much so that he noticed a mark of something reflecting on his shoe. He hoped he hadn't stepped in something on the way in, as one of staff smiled at him on her way past.

The reception lady seemed pleasant enough, dressed in an off white top, the same as the other ladies in the office behind her. She asked him to take a seat, which he did. Even the seats were white. As he was sitting there waiting, a man walked past carrying cleaning utensils; he stopped and observed Andy as though he had just seen an old friend. Andy couldn't place him.

"Hello, my name is John; I'm a cleaner here." he said. Andy nodded back a greeting, "Are you here for a consultation?" John asked. He was in his early sixties, by the look of him. He moved around with a smooth gracefulness more normally associated with ball room dancers than cleaners.

"An interview for the chef's position. Do I know you from somewhere?" Andy asked. John was looking at him in a way that suggested he did.

"I feel as though I do." John smiled, "Good luck with the interview." John added, before going about his duties.

After a few minutes, Susan, a woman in her early forties appeared. She led him through to a room with more white chairs in it. She asked Andy to take a seat. The other person in the room was Eric, a clean shaven middle aged looking man, wearing a white chef jacket with the French flag on its pocket.

"Hi, thank you for coming. I'm Sue, this is Eric. We like to keep the interviews here fairly informal Andrew. Can I get you a coffee?"

"Hi, oh no, I'm fine thanks." replied Andy.

Everyone, so far, seemed too *posh* to be working in what appeared to be a hospital of some kind.

"So, tell me Andrew, do you know anything about the Haven?" Susan asked. Andy had *googled* the Haven the previous night.

"Well, I did do a bit of research. I looked at your web-site. Yes, it seems like a really interesting place; you use alternative methods in dealing with illness."

"Good. Yes that's right. We use *alternative* health treatments and methods. Also, Dominic, the owner of the Haven, is a trained psychologist. He holds psychotherapy sessions...amongst other things."

"Ah yes, I saw that as well." Andy said.

"Hmm yes, the good thing is, he only charges the people that can afford to pay." Sue added.

*So far everything seemed perfect.*

"What kind of hours are you working at the moment?" Eric asked, in good English, but with a good hint of French accent.

"Well, quite long days really. It varies a bit, but usually  from 10 am till around 10 pm, with a break in-between."

"The dreaded split-shifts. Oh I remember them well." Eric nodded with a smile, "Here, we only work till around 4 o'clock. There is the occasional evening as well, if there's an event on; though there's probably only three or four of those a year."

Andy unsuccessfully tried to suppress a big grin. *Those hours were great.* Because of the grin, Andy thought he may as well come clean.

"I have to be honest, that was one of the

things that attracted me to the job."

Eric was a seasoned campaigner himself and knew exactly where he was coming from.

"I understand. There are much worse hours than these." He whispered the next line, "That's a big reason why I am here."

Sue heard him and smiled a little. She said, "The most impressive thing about the Haven cafe is that it is a place that uses nothing but fresh organic ingredients. Absolutely no frozen food."

"And no tins." Eric added, "We don't even have a tin-opener."

"We grow quite a lot of our own vegetables." Susan added, "It fits in with the concept of natural healing."

"Yes, I did see that on the job advert and also on the web-site. That really appealed to me." replied Andy, glad that he did some research. But in all honesty, if they had told him everything was tinned and frozen, he would have said *that* was good.

"Well, we only use the best produce, it is *mostly* organic, that costs twice as much." Eric said, smiling. Andy smiled back.

"Does that mean you're not too strict about the profit margins? I saw your menu on the web-site and the prices were not...."

"Extortionate?" suggested Eric.

"Well, not much higher than the average café." Andy explained.

Susan added more detail. "Dominic doesn't look at just the profits. He sees that health and well-being comes from within. What you eat is the starting point. He's willing to sacrifice making a profit with that concept in mind."

"We are here to make food for the patients, but besides that, anyone else can walk into the café." Eric said, "I have looked through your references and you have worked at some good places; busy places." Eric knew very well, the value of working at busy places; it suggested that you could generally cope under pressure. Some couldn't.

"Yes, several. Some quite varied places. Some of which have been a similar style to the food here at the Haven."

"I noticed you have worked at the *Stone house.* I spent a year there, what...seven or eight years ago. Was Daniel running it when you were there?" Eric asked.

"Yes he was. I think he's still there now." *Always good if there is a common point of reference.*

"Do you think you would be alright with this menu?" Susan asked. She already viewed Andrew as the leading candidate; he seemed fairly *normal* for a chef. Not a prima donna.

"Oh, absolutely yes."

"Are there any questions you would like to ask?"

"Yes, would I be able to come up with my

own specials and have input in the menus?" Andy asked. He knew that this question was a killer and suggested enthusiasm that may or may not exist.

"Yes, to both questions of course, we encourage that." Susan replied, "What is your notice period Andrew?"

"Actually, the place where I am at the moment has just been sold, so I could probably start whenever needed really."

"The last full time chef we had got ill, then he suddenly got better and left. Eric is in the kitchen at the moment, but he's only really *filling in* whilst we find someone. He might go back to working part-time after that." Susan glanced over to Eric to see if he confirmed that or not.

"Possibly." Was Eric's rather non-commital response. He didn't mind covering for now, but as soon as they had found a replacement, he probably wouldn't stick around for long.

Susan talked through all the usual stuff. She outlined the standard holiday pay entitlements and after a few more standard questions she said. "Great, well that's the interview over. Nice to have met you and thank you for coming along. We will contact you in the next few days to let you know whether you have been successful."

Andy got up from his chair. The sunlight was streaming in through the large tinted windows. He shook the hands of Susan and Eric and then left the interview room, trying not to blow it by knocking something over on the way out. This job seemed almost too good to be true. He needed a bit of good fortune and he glanced up towards the heavens as though to ask whether this was it.

As he walked back to his car, he passed a man with shoulder length hair, dressed in loose fitting white cotton clothes. He was about to get into the white Range Rover and he was accompanied by two rather serious looking, shaven headed gorillas that seemed to stick out like a sore thumb in this place of *supposed* tranquillity. Whoever it was payed him no attention. *Nice car though.*

The rust spots on the old Ford looked more noticable, given its present company. As he drove past the Range Rover he felt the driver turn his nose up at him, even if he didn't actually see it. He left the tarmac, joined the rough track for thirty seconds and then turned back on to the main road and...reality.

# 7

Andy woke very early the next morning; he hadn't planned to, but at least today there was no strange dream to recount. Just as he was thinking about setting off to work, he got a call from Mark, the manager, telling him not to come in as there was some kind of appraisal by the new owners and that they wouldn't be serving food. Andy asked if he would still be getting paid; Mark was non commital on that; he neither knew nor cared.

Andy wondered whether to call Jane and ask if he could spend time with the kids. The last time he had tried to switch days she hadn't let him see them for two weeks as a punishment, so he didn't bother. Instead he called Mick and asked if he wanted to hang out for a while. Mick was a big fan of both cowboy/western films and martial arts films, or to be more accurate, he was *obsessed* by them.

An undubbed Bruce lee film played on the tv as Andy entered Mick's flat.

"Do you understand what they are saying?"

Andy asked him.

"Don't need to. Actions speak louder than words. But I do know a few lines of Mandarin from watching it with the subtitles on."

"Tell me one then."

"....pijiu."

"What does that mean?"

"Beer."

"Is that it?"

"More or less. Just in case I ever go to china." Mick explained and then he changed the subject, “You lied at the interview then?”

“Lied? No I didn’t lie.”

“You gave them the old *specials board bullshit.*”

“Well, yeah. I sounded enthusiastic about the menus as well.”

“So you lied.”

“Look, if I had said, I *only want this job because the hours are good,* they wouldn't offer it me.”

“That French guy knows the score.” Mick turned his attention back to the Bruce Lee film. “Who do you think is the best Bruce?” he asked.

“You mean the best at kung fu?”

“No, the best *Bruce*, as in the best person called *Bruce.*”

“I can only think of a couple...Bruce Lee and Bruce Springsteen.” Andy said.

“There are a few more...Bruce Campbell.”

“Who is that?”

“He was in the *Evil Dead* films.”

"Oh yeah, him. Maybe top ten."

"Bruce Dickinson, Iron Maiden."

"He's not in the running."

"Na suppose not, bit of a nob-head...allegedly."

"Bruce Forsyth?" Andy suggested.

*"Good game, good game."*

"What about *Robert the Bruce*, the Scottish bloke."

"Yeah maybe, except that he's *The Bruce*. His name is actually Robert...sadly, we can't count him in. Not sure what he did anyway."

"Don't say that to a Scotsman. He's something like a saint up in Scotland."

"What did he do then?" Mick asked.

"I have no idea, but it must have been pretty good. Invented tossing the caber?"

"Scotland doesn't produce many greats; who else is there?"

"Sean Connery and Andy Murray, that's about it. What about *Bruce Wayne*, Batman." Andy offered.

"Not a real person. Has to be a real person, ....it probably is Bruce Lee." Mick pointed to the television, "I mean look at that, he's just kicked the crap out of ten guys in five seconds. That's 0.5 of a second per bad guy."

"Wait.... Bruce Willis."

"Yeah, John McClain, good call. Now, if we were watching *Die Hard* right now we might say *he* was the best." Mick said as he shot imaginary enemy's with his finger, "Yippee-Ki-Ay motherfucker!!"

"It's a pity about him and what happened. They are shoving him in any old crap just to have his name on the poster."

Andy and Mick sat and watched for a few more minutes in silence until Mick had finalised his list.

"Ok, top three in this order. Third, Bruce Willis, second Springsteen and first Bruce Lee."

"Quite unusual name for a Chinese bloke though, *Bruce.*" Andy said.

"I think he was half American." Mick said.

"You know quite a lot of semi-useless information."

Mick opened a can of beer. "Pijiu. You see, proof that alcohol does not destroy your brain cells."

"Perhaps not *all* of them." Andy's said, as his phone beeped. He checked it and saw a new e-mail from the Haven, "Bloody hell, they are offering me the job." he said, moderately surprised.

"That's great man. When do they want you to start? How much money? Answer the second question first."

"Decent money....beginning of next week. That's cool, because of the pay off we're getting, for once, I'm actually coming out ahead."

"You see. I told you things were gonna change. Hi–Ya!" Mick said, as he performed an unimpressive kung-fu style chop.

◆ ◆ ◆

Andy went to the supermarket after visiting Mick. He didn't need anything, but felt *out of sorts* and wanted to go somewhere else before he went home. As he was walking down an aisle, he saw what looked like Jane at the other end of it. She was with some bloke or other. *Perhaps that was the infamous Mr Wonderful.* Andy stopped in his tracks. His heart leapt and blood pumped more quickly through his veins. They had their backs to him, but he recognised her shape. Mr Wonderful, or Rick, was laughing and joking. *What a great guy.* Andy thought about turning around and leaving. He didn't actually need anything. No, he decided to turn around, but then head down the next aisle and head them off, if he timed it right, at the freezers. He turned. His heart pumping. Adrenalin kicked in. He had no idea what he would do or say when he came face to face with them but he was going to do *something.*

"Well, look at the happy couple." he said as he turned the corner. The blonde woman turned to face him. It wasn't Jane.

"Excuse me?" she said. The man accompanying her was a work colleague of hers and definately not Rick. "Do I know you?"

Andy was standing there confused. He let his hard expression soften.

"Sorry. I though you were someone else."

The man that was with her put a hand on her back and guided her past this strange aggressive shopper. They moved on beyond the freezers. Andy still had some adrenalin in his system. *Did he feel better or worse that it wasn't them?* He slowly walked away and looked at products he had no intention of buying.

# 8

Andy woke up when the sun was just thinking about starting to rise. He rarely got up *this* early, and he hadn't slept well. He was not feeling nervous exactly, but he wanted to make his first day at the Haven a good one: make a good impression. He had gone to bed early at 11:00 pm, but that hadn't payed off because he just lay in bed for over an hour, his body clock refusing to accept that it was sleep time. All he did was ruminate. On five hours sleep he felt ok, or at least he thought he did.  He drank the last sip of coffee, had a very quick shower and shave and, after checking himself in the mirror, he left his flat, hoping that today would be the first chapter of a better phase in is life.

◆ ◆ ◆

The Haven looked even more impressive the next time that he saw it; rays of the morning sun cascading through the canopy of trees before glinting on the extensive glass and white walls of the building. He was also quietly impressed that they had offered him the job so quickly. He supposed the key to this promptness might be Eric, and the mutual place of work they shared. Not to mention the fact that Eric wanted to get someone else quickly, so that the pressure was off him. Whatever the reason was, Andy knew that he was good at his job and reliable and would do alright for them. He hadn't been gifted the job… it was down to his experience and merit, *and fate?*

He walked down the gravel path, which crunched under his feet, to the entrance. Inside, he asked the receptionist for Susan, who duly appeared. They greeted. Susan seemed more serious than she did at the interview, but still pleasant enough. The ones you had to watch were the ones that had made a complete personality transformation from interview to day one, knowing full well that you had given up the other job.

"Before we go to the kitchen, I'll give you the guided tour. Just to give you a feel for the place before you start doing any cooking. Eric is going to be in there for at least a couple of weeks to show you the ropes. Follow me please." Susan said. Andy followed her to the starting point of the mini tour around the facility.

"Place seems even bigger on the inside today." Andy said. Susan was moving at a brisk a pace as possible, without rushing. Her time obviously had value. She opened the first door, explaining as she did so that these first few rooms were used for pilates, massage and acupuncture, "I'm not sure what *pilates* is, although I have heard of it." Andy said.

"People think that it's a new concept but it's not." Susan said, then, whispering as though this was a secret, "It's trendy and a fad at the moment, but any exercise is good, especially for the older ones." She continued moving on and opening doors further down the corridor, allowing Andy a brief peek inside each room.

"So, you employ a lot of staff, with all these treatment rooms?" Andy asked. He tried to sound interested. He was, a little.

"No, we don't employ the staff for this part of the Haven: we lease these rooms out to practitioners."

With the ground floor ticked off, they headed off up the wide staircase. Up on the first floor, there were heavy, expensive looking wooden doors. In this part of the building, the lighting was different and subtle, creating a contrasting mood. Downstairs was functional and bright, this was....tranquil. Susan opened the first door.

"This is one of the treatment rooms." Inside were tables that looked both expensive and comfortable to lie on. There were movable devices the like of which Andy had never seen before.

Complex looking things, some of which looked like props from a sci-fi film.

"Interesting. Not exactly NHS by the looks of it." Andy said.

"Not quite, no. These particular machines utilize oscillating frequencies, using rare and expensive crystals." They passed by two similar treatment rooms and then a white door that seemed to lead to a seperate area. It had symbols on it Andy didn't recognise, "That is Dominic's office. I can't show you in there." Not *won't,* but *can't.* Susan opened the next door further down, "This is the newest machine we have. It's the latest breaking technology here, the only one in existence."

"It looks expensive,...what does it do?" Andy asked. This peice of equipment looked like nothing else. It still had cardboard packing on parts of it and blue tape.

"We haven't actually used it yet." Susan produced a large, thick manual for the machine from under the desk and held it up for Andy to see, "This is the instruction book, if and when I get time to read it." Next, Susan showed him the patient's rooms, there were four in total, "The machines that you saw in the treatment rooms are movable, so we can move them in to the patients if need be. Some of the patients we get are very ill, some only have mild ailments. At the moment we have just the one residental patient."

Andy was now genuinely interested in the tour; this place seemed like another world, hidden away. Susan had slowed down a little as she showed him the patient treatment rooms. It all seemed rather informal up here and not much like a hospital ward. The tour was over. He had seen all there was to see, with the exeption of the room beyond the white door, and they headed downstairs to the kitchen and café. In the café, John the cleaner was working on polishing the floor. Susan showed Andy the dining area and then the coffee machine area. John removed his earphones, something he very rarely did. He listened to Pink Floyd most of the time, though not exclusively. He looked at Andy, once again, like he had just seen an old school friend or a long lost family member. Andy, once again, thought it slightly unusual.

Susan introduced them both. “This is Andrew the new chef. Andrew this is John.”

Andy actually checked his own hair in the reflection of the coffee machine with his hand, because the way John was looking at him made him think he had some hair sticking up on end. John had an *unusual, subtle* smile on his face as he removed the blue latex gloves from his right then left hands.

“Pleased to meet you again.” Andy said.

“You too. I’m glad you got the job. I had a strong feeling you would.” John replied.

John extended his right hand to Andy's. They had the standard handshake, then, in a smooth movement John placed his left hand also on Andy's right hand, just for a brief second or two. Andy felt a small jolt of what seemed to be static electricity pass through his entire body. It wasn't unpleasant and Andy put it down to a build up of static that John had accumulated from the buffering machine. John looked straight ahead for a few moments as though he was trying to recollect something, then he nodded and continued working on the floor.

The introductions were then over and Andy got changed into his chef's uniform in possibly the cleanest changing room he'd ever seen.

Andy hadn't had the amount of sleep he usually got, but inspite of that, the rest of the first day started well. Eric was pleased to have some help, but he didn't seem in *too* big a rush to get Andy to the point where he could be left on his own. The way they did things was different to what Andy was used to, but nothing he couldn't handle and adapt to. At lunchtime the café was steady rather than busy, plus there was only one patient, so it was all quite relaxed and slow paced. The only time that there was any commotion was around 1:30 pm when a lot of chatter was heard coming from the dining room.

"Here comes Dominic." Eric said. From the kitchen, Andy could see the guy who was getting into the white Range Rover a few days earlier. He was clad all in white again, and this time he had an entourage of half a dozen people following him. From a distance, it looked like they were flocking around him like groupies to a rock star.

“So that’s the owner?” Andy asked.

“Yep, plus his hangers on of course.” Eric said.

“Does he ever come in here?”

“Rarely. All he ever has at lunch is soup. If he particularly likes it, he might come in and tell you. He's been in to see me just the once. That's the way I like it.”

Dom sat at the table in the centre of the café. At this point in the day, John, the cleaner, came to the kitchen side door, he thanked Eric and Andy for the sandwich that he'd had for lunch and then he told Andy that he had to go now, but would hopefully speak more with him tomorrow. Andy was pleased that all the staff seemed to be nice enough. He had a theory, quite commonly held, especially by Mick, that wherever you go there is always one asshole to deal with. He thought he may have struck gold with this new place.

# 9

*Dominic Pearce. That is the person who they are going to be talking to.* Dom checked his appearance in the mirror. The local regional news team was doing a small piece on the Haven and its owner with the ground-breaking alternative healing methods. This could be the exposure that *really* put them on the map. This could be the start of something *really* big. To Dom though, it was more than anything else, a chance for more adulation and attention. Any other benefits were secondary. The reason he had spent half a million pounds renovating the formerly derelict building, now *the Haven*, was to erect a never ending supply of fuel to bolster his hungry ego. He hadn't really been expecting to make money as well, but if that was the case, then even better.

*The limelight.* Here it was in the form of a reporter with a small outdoor camera unit. Dom made sure his metaphorical mask was a perfect fit before he joined the news crew at the front of the building. The newscaster was a woman in her late twenties, who had worked her way up from tea-girl. She'd already briefed Dom on what type of questions she would ask and told him roughly how long it would take. She didn't really like/dislike Dom or feel any affinity to what he did; but she had a practiced way of disguising this.

It would all be edited together later. Dom was tempted to ask if he could sit in on the editing, just so he could keep in all the best bits of himself, but decided against it: they probably would have refused.

When Dom was standing in the right spot, just at the right angle in front of the Haven, the crew signaled "*action*" the reporter's expression changed to a smile and she began the interview.

"Dominic, you are establishing a growing reputation here at the Haven. Tell me, when you first conceived the idea of this facility, what did you set out to achieve?"

Dom looked straight into the camera for a moment, then back at the interviewer. "It started out as a project of mine, two years ago. I became aware of particular methods, *non-conventional methods,* shall we say, to heal many different illnesses."

"Reports say that some patients, given no hope of a cure, have had their symptoms just go away. Simply disappear."

"Yes that's true. Our success is growing. From the ground up, I designed and built the Haven to be a facility that took modern science and merged it with ancient and forgotten methods."

"Is it true that the use of crystals plays a big part in some of your procedures?"

"The rare crystals do play a significant part, yes, but also....*the power of the mind."*

"Do you mean faith healing? That *is* practiced as part of some of the procedures here." the interviewer asked.

"Not exactly just that, though that is a gift some people do possess. More like man and machine coming together to help people....in harmony."

"So you can't have one without the other. The machines that you use for treatments are quite unique aren't they?"

"Indeed, yes they are. Pioneering, I don't want to say *technology,* I prefer the term *advancements.* I, or we, have developed and manufactured them and are the only facility worldwide that uses them, at present."

"Are they a closely guarded secret?"

"I wouldn't say closely guarded, but they are unique."

"It sounds fascinating and very exciting Dominic. Do you think there is scope for expansion? Will we see more *Havens* cropping up in the near future?"

"That's not something I've really considered. My main focus is on doing the best we can here.

But…you never know." He gave the camera a smile as though he knew something the viewers didn't.

The interviewer thanked Dom for his time. The slot had been filmed and the crew called it a wrap. Of course, Dom *had* thought about expanding and having several versions of the Haven throughout the country. More Haven's equalled more attention.

The cameraman looked across to the soundman as they began to close things up and get all the equipment back to the van.

"What do you reckon to that guy?" he asked.

"Bit of a clown."

"Rich clown." the cameraman said.

◆ ◆ ◆

Andy was satisfied with his first day at the Haven. A quarter past 4pm and that's it...finished for the day. All he had to think about now was the date he had tonight and also...how he was so very out of practice with the dating scene. He didn't suppose it had changed much in the last decade, just be yourself and all that. This was set up by Mick though, so goodness only knew what she, Sally, would be like.

The butterflies kicked in about an hour before he was due to meet Sally. Just a couple of drinks though, *what harm was there in that*?

Five minutes before 8:00 pm Andy was waiting outside the local cinema for Sally, who turned up at five minutes past 8:00 pm. The closer she got, the nicer she looked. Mick hadn't lied about that bit.

"Hi, you're Andy?"

"Hi, yes. That means you are Sally."

"Or Sal if you prefer. Nice to meet you. Sorry I'm a couple of minutes late."

"No problem. So, what would you like to do?"

"Well, the drink you mentioned sounds like a good plan."

"Where do you fancy going? There is a decent bar just around the corner."

"Yeah great, let's go there then."

They headed off in the direction of the bar. *So far so good. How much conversation should he make?* He didn't want to seem dour by saying too little.

"So this is your night off then?" she asked, on the way.

"Well it wasn't, I mean it is now. I swapped jobs... I just started at the new place today."

"Oh, that's good, no more working with Mick then?"

"No, not sure whether that's a good or a bad thing. No, he's a good guy...when he wants to be."

"I've known Mick since school. He was a few years above me." Sally commented.

"Was he? I bet he was just as mad back then as

well."

"Yeah he was. Pretty funny guy, or so he thinks. Mind you, a few of the girls did used to fancy him."

"Oh. Ha."

"Not me though."

Andy got the hint that she probably did. *Was she one of Mick's ex's?* They entered the bar and approached the barman. *She did seem quite nice and definitely not a Russian weightlifter.*

"So what would you like to drink? he asked.

"A glass of wine I think...dry white please." *This was a good sign; a weightlifter might possibly have wanted a pint of ale*. Andy ordered the wine and a bottle of beer for himself.

"Would you like to sit down or?"

"Let's go over there." she suggested. They moved to a table on one side of the bar. Thankfully, she seemed to be taking the lead, "So, how long did you work with Mick?"

"Too long! About a year. Actually, I'm joking, we get on really well."

"Yeah he said so."

"So what do you do?" Andy asked. *First question out of the way.*

"I work in a school, I'm a teaching assistant."

"Ah. You must have patience then."

"Yes I suppose so. I'm at college as well...part time."

"You keep busy then by the sounds of it."

At one end of the bar, a group started picking up their instruments and switching on equipment.

"Oh, there's a band on." Sally said.

"Do you know them?"

"No. I wonder what kind of music they play? Go on you guess first."

"Ok. ...Punk."

"Oh no, really? They don't look like Punks. Do those bands even still exist?"

"Ok, seriously...Blues." Andy guessed.

"Ok. I'll guess *Rock*, not Heavy Metal, just like *normal* Rock."

"You mean like the Eagles?"

"What did they sing?"

"Hotel California?"

"I think I've heard of that."

"Anyway, it looks like they are about to start." The band started playing...a Blues song about waking up in the morning feeling bad, "Looks like I won."

"Is this Blues? Is it not Rock? How can you tell?"

"It's fairly similar, except they sound a bit more miserable. Always complaining about something. Well, actually I cheated a bit. I knew it was Blues because I saw a poster on the way in saying it was *blues night* on Thursdays."

"Hey you cheater!" Sally said, laughing. She had to raise her voice, "A bit loud!"

They were pretty good and as they listened, the bar filled up and got a bit livelier. Andy went and got another round of drinks. After a few songs, the band took a break for a few minutes. *The date was going smoothly*, so far at least. His confidence had been knocked by Jane, well, not just knocked but hit with a sledgehammer. That didn't mean every woman was going to reject him and that's what he needed to realise. *Women play by different rules*, Mick had said. Jane's issues went somewhat deeper than what lay on the surface, but that didn't stop him from feeling bad about being the scapegoat.

After the second drink, they set off for another bar. Outside, some leaves were just beginning to fall and were swirling around in the light breeze that pleasantly greeted them outside.

"Do you go out a lot?" Sally asked.

"Not a lot."

"When was the last time you went out around town then?"

"Hmmm...it's about a year ago." Andy said.

"Wow, you really don't go out much."

"Well I used to. I mean...before the kids were born."

"Oh, I didn't know you had kids."

Andy sensed the very faintest glimmer of disapproval, no matter how much she was trying to disguise it. Mick obviously hadn't told her. "Yes two."

"How old are they?"

"One is four, the other is now seven."

"You must have started young!"

"Well, yeah I guess so."

They arrived at the next bar and went inside. Sally insisted on buying the next round of drinks, she went and ordered and the two sat at a table. It was a lot quieter in this bar. All the furniture was wood and crafted from barrels and other objects. There was just the jukebox in the other room providing background noise, so the conversation was clearer and felt more focused.

"So, you split from their mum a while ago?"

"A few months ago."

"Must be difficult."

"It has its moments. I was used to seeing the kids every day. That's the hardest part." Andy tried to be honest, without going into too much detail that she probably didn't need to know or want to know.

"Is there no chance of you getting back with your ex-wife? *Were* you married?"

"It doesn't look like it, and yes we were married."

Sally was looking at Andy's right hand "Is that your wedding ring?" Andy looked at the ring like he was surprised to see it on there.

"Ah, yes. I moved it onto the other hand, after we split up."

"You're not ready to take it off completely yet

then."

"Phew. I never really thought of it like that. I suppose I should now." Andy had moved the ring before he had found out about *Mr wonderful* on the scene, with the thought that it might possibly swap hands back to the left once again.

"Sorry I'm being nosey! It's a nice ring anyway."

The ring was just a plain gold band. Andy noticed the tone of the date had changed slightly...*or was is massively?*

"Anyway, tell me more about yourself." Andy said, changing the subject. The beer had made him more relaxed. Sally obliged and told him a lot, but nothing of any real depth or meaning. She avoided any more serious subjects with a subtle skill.

Two hours later and they were back in the first bar, the band were playing their last song for the night. It had gone smoothly and this girl really was pleasant. The several drinks they'd had were making the conversation flow and also making Sally a little less co-ordinated. Reaching for her bag, she accidentally knocked over a glass which broke on the table. A drop of blood dripped onto the table and Andy instinctively reached out to take Sally's hand to survey the damage. A bar staff member came over to clean up the broken glass. Andy checked the palm of Sally's hand. There was no sign of a cut; *must be on the back of her hand.* He gently turned it over. *Nothing there either.* There were definately a few drops of blood on the table, but no sign of a cut.

"You seem fine." he said.

"Clumsy, ha ha." Sally said. They got up and left the bar, "That band was pretty good."

"Yeah they were."

"Can you believe it's nearly midnight?"

"I know tonight has gone quickly."

"What time you up in the morning?" she asked.

"Quarter to seven."

"Ah, are we past your bed time?"

"I suppose, these early starts are a bit of a novelty." They both told each other what a nice time they'd had. Sally lived in the opposite direction to him; they didn't share a taxi...they did share a brief kiss. Andy told her he would give her a call in a few days. He decided to walk back to his flat, feeling a slightly warm glow as he did so. He couldn't tell whether that was the beer or optimism about Sally. Maybe a bit of both.

# 10

Rick, the man re-named *Mr Wonderful,* by Mick was the eldest of two brothers. Not spoilt by his mother and treated not treated badly by his father. All through school he was always a little big bigger than his classmates; he being one of the oldest in the year. From that young age, he used that size difference to his advantage in every way that he could think of. Bullying the smaller kids for money or just for fun was one of his favourite pastimes.

Not particularly skilled at football, he was in the school team based on his physical presence. He once fractured an opposing player's leg with a particularly nasty challenge, without displaying the slightest hint of remorse. In fact, as the other kid was being stretchered off, the team manager detected the faint outline of a smile on Rick's lips.

He liked crime and action films. No sci-fi though; he lacked the imagination for that. He didn't read books.

He had once slept with his brother's ex-girlfriend, just a week or two after they had split up. When his brother had found out and confronted him, all he said in his defence was.

"You weren't together."

The fact that he was instrumental in splitting up this young family did not tug on his conscience. It just didn't register. Put simply, what Rick wanted, he wanted and to hell with the consequences. This one dimensional way of thinking and living had served him well so far in life. He had a good paying job, a new BMW car and an attractive new girlfriend. She would suit him well, for the time being at least. Jane having kids was not an ideal situation, but what the hell. In two or three years he may well have moved on. It's not like he was planning to marry the woman, not with someone elses kids in tow.

The news had come through that he had been expecting: the new job offer was concrete. He would become the new area manager for the company that he worked for. It would mean relocating, but that was no problem: Jane would come with him, she had said. If she didn't come, then it would take a while to find a replacement, which would have been inconvenient, but so far, the lavish attention he had heaped upon her was paying dividends... she was eating out of his hand. These married woman were easy pickings if they were the right type and felt under appreciated.

He called Jane to tell her the good news. She had responded positively. So far she had only seen the good side of him; the other side was yet to come. All in good time.

# 11

The next day Andy woke up at the sound of the alarm. Thankfully, he felt no ill effects from the several drinks he'd had the previous night: he wasn't a big drinker and often felt it pretty bad the next day. *A lightweight*, Mick often called him. He replayed some of the date as he got dressed. His mind was fully occupied, as usual, but refreshingly, it wasn't all negative today.

The second day at work started off well, Eric was already there when he arrived and Andy felt he was quickly developing a rapport with him. The job was slowly falling into place and didn't seem too stressful. Andy did hope that Eric would stay on at least part time, because he was good to have around and just generally a cool guy. They worked in tandam pretty well and made a good two man team.

After the lunch service, John popped his head into the kitchen and enquired whether either Andy or Eric would like a drink of tea or coffee.

"How are you settling in?" John asked.

"Well, so far so good, everyone seems nice enough." Andy replied.

"Do you have five minutes?" John asked.

"Sure. What is it?"

"Just a quick chat…if you don't mind."

Andy and John sat at a table in the now almost empty café. Eric continued clearing away in the kitchen whilst also chatting on his phone in French.

"I'm going to tell you something that you're going to find a little…*out there*." John said.

"…Ok."

"Have you felt any different…since yesterday?"

"Different? In what way different?"

"Do you believe in anything, let's say….*supernatural*?"

"You have lost me a bit here."

"It's going to be quite difficult to explain. Just bear with me because this *is* going to sound a little….weird. You have a gift."

"What?"

"A special talent….so to speak."

"I'm really not following you. I should probably get back and help Eric…"

"I know you have a talent and you don't realize it yet. I know, because I passed it on to you."

"A talent for doing what?" Andy thought that this was the guy who was going to spoil the job, the one asshole in every place.

"You can heal people."

"Ok...look I really need to be getting back. Thanks for the coffee." Andy smiled thinly, got up and went back in to the kitchen. "Is that guy all there?" he asked Eric.

"Who...John? Yes, top man, he's been here a while, nice fella. Why do you ask?"

"Aw, nothing really...he just said something a bit odd."

"Don't worry about John; he's always been fine with me. Very down to Earth."

"Ok....maybe I misheard him."

They finished clearing down and then started packing away, ready for a fresh start the next day. Just as Andy was taking the last load of crockery out of the dishwasher, he noticed that one of the glasses had broken whilst being in there. *Must have had a crack in it.* Then he had a flashback to the previous night with Sally and the broken glass. *Blood...but no cut.* He dismissed that thought, as it made no sense, said goodbye to Eric and drove home.

◆ ◆ ◆

That night he felt the need for some familiarity and called around to his former workplace. He stood at the kitchen's back door and waited for Mick to appear. he wasn't long.

“So how did it go?” Mick asked.

“The job?”

“No, the date, let’s get our priorities right, you can tell me about the job later.”

“Yeah, it was ok. Nice enough girl.”

“Where did you take her?”

“A couple of bars in town.”

“Cool. Take her home afterwards?”

“No, I put her in a taxi.”

“Ah, you should’ve invited her back to yours.”

“For coffee?" Mick shook his head, "On the first date?”

“She would’ve been up for it.”

“How do you know?”

“Just trust me, she would’ve.”

“So you’re telling me you set me up with a ….."

“No dude, but….she’s not exactly shy in that department either.”

“I see.”

“Come on pal, you’re both adults. Did you get on alright anyway?”

“She seemed alright, we got on quite well. I said I’d text her in a day or two.”

“Cool, well it was a day or two ago, why don’t you send her a text now? Let me go and do a bit of work, be back in five.”

Andy sat and wondered if he really did want another date with Sally. Then, on automatic pilot, he sent her a text message asking if she fancied meting up again. As he waited, his mind flitted back and forth between Jane telling him they might be moving, the date with Sally and also the odd conversation he'd had with John previously that day. *What had he said, healing powers*? At least if that guy was a nut case, he would be avoidable for the majority of the time. Mick returned after about ten minutes.

"Have you texted her yet? What did you put?"

"Just to see if she wanted to go for a drink again sometime."

"And what did she say?"

"Nothing yet, she's not replied. You sure I'm not rushing things?"

Mick shook his head. "No, they can't reply too soon, it's all part of the game."

"It does feel a bit like a game, and I've forgotten all the rules."

"That's why I'm pushing you a bit pal. Think of me as your coach. Call me *Pep Guardiola.*"

"Yeah, well I don't feel like I'm exactly in the Premier league at the minute."

There was the sound of a mobile phone message being received. Andy picked up his phone and studied the newly received text message for a few seconds. It read...*Hi, had good tym on thur. Not sure if going out agen good idea tho. Sal x*

"Well?" Mick asked.

"You read it."

Andy passed his phone to Mick who read the

message.

"Strange. Ask her why not."

"Na. Forget it."

"No go on. I'll do it then, from your phone. She said she liked you."

"Suit yourself."

"I'll just ask *any reason why*?"

"Go on then…but that's *all* you put."

Mick typed and sent the message, then gave the phone back to Andy. Not long after the phone beeped again and Andy checked the reply.

*Hi sorry it's just that you have kids.*

"What did she say?" Mick asked. Andy passed the phone once again to Mick who read the reply, "You're kidding. That's harsh. Silly cow, what a bitch."

"Whatever. She is obviously shallow at least."

"Well. Yeah. To be honest dude, I probably set you up with her to get you back into the swing of things again… you can look on that date as just practice."

"Yeah, I'm with you. You tried."

"So how is the new job?" Mick asked.

"It's alright, so far. Everyone seems ok. One guy, the cleaner, may be a bit of an oddball."

"There's always one." Mick said, flatly.

# 12

Andy had not gotten used to driving to his former home, then waiting outside and not actually going inside. It felt especially bad with the kids in the car, a gut wrench every time. Similarly as traumatic was the icy cold reception he now got from Jane. Even so, he *had* still thought that there was some chance that they could resolve their differences. He *had* thought that although the connection between them had been severed from her side, it would take some work to repair, but it could be done...it wasn't mission impossible. Their relationship hadn't been perfect; whose was? But now it was like a completely different person was answering the door.

Andy *had* been kicking himself for making accusations of infidelity. Had that turned any love that she had to hate? The answer, as he had found out recently was a resounding *no*. He had been totally correct with his accusation. A neighbour, stirring up trouble for her own entertainment, rather than from any loyalty to Andy, had told him that Jane had a *boyfriend*. When Andy had questioned Jane the next day, she'd replied in a official sounding tone straight out of a court room, *"I'm not confirming or denying anything."* This knowledge had been the game changer. The possibility of a reconciliation had blasted out of sight, like a rocket heading deep into space, never to be seen again.

The house was rented, and in her name, though he never imagined that would become an issue. Couples split up all the time, but with two small children? Surely any problems could be sorted out before a complete split had to take place. The ramifications would be enormous. Not in this case. Not with an extra player entering stage right. This wasn't delayed post natal depression or anything else for that matter; her head had been turned by what she *supposed* was a better deal. Andy *supposed* that she had been wearing some sort of mask all along, for all the entire time that he was with her. That's what it felt like. Now she had no need for it. She came out of the door, arms folded with what could only be described as a *vacant* look on her face. A formal look you might give to the train inspector as they checked your ticket. This time she had something more to say on the subject of moving. First she asked Andy if he was alright, then she ushered the kids inside, before saying.

"There's a *stronger* possibility we might be moving." Andy glimpsed the shadow of a male in the house behind. "There's now a pretty good chance we will be doing."

"Surely that's a bad idea? The kids are settled here."

"It's a fresh start for everyone."

"How far away? 200 miles you said?"

"It's *only just* 200 miles."

"*Only just* 200, oh well, that's alright then! Why go so far away?" Andy got agitated.

"I'm not discussing it any further today, if you can't be reasonable, this conversation is over."

She turned to go back inside the house. The kids had gone up to the window and were waving at their dad as he stood rooted to the spot for a few seconds. They were still smiling, unaware of his pain. He wanted to bang on the door. Do something extreme. Instead, for their sake, he smiled and waved at the kids before getting back into the Ford and driving away.

# 13

Day three at the Haven. Day three was where things usually fell into place, more or less. Andy had lost count of how many new jobs he had started, he could have worked it out given the inclination, but day three was when he had generally gotten used to where everything was kept and also gotten a handle on the menu, without having the need to check it every time an order came on. He was offered agency work once, but it meant sometimes working just one solitary day at a completely new place and set-up. Constantly opening fridges and freezers, trying to find things, basically no less than a nightmare situation. The customers didn't care whether it was your first day or not, they just wanted feeding in a reasonable time. He had tried it just once as a favour to a former friend, but rapidly dismissed with the idea as too stressful. Day three was usually the breakthrough day and it did start well enough: it was steady during service rather than busy and all the orders were not complicated.

As there was just the two of them, he was quickly getting to know Eric a little better, and the more he did, the more interesting a character he seemed. He looked to be in his mid fifties and was undoubtedly French....Andy had detected the accent the first time he had spoken, but had not wanted to assume anything in case he offended Eric by getting the wrong nationality. He had once massively offended a New Zealand native by assuming he was Australian. Andy didn't see anything wrong with Australians, at least not enough to provoke the response he got.

Eric was a Frenchman who liked the English and also liked living here. Andy supposed, in that respect, he was a rarity. He remained faithful to the white French cigarettes and seemed to go through quite a few of them. He was someone that took everything in his stride, as long as he could have his cigarette breaks, you could throw virtually anything at him and he would remain unruffled.

"Have you ever tried to quit? I managed to do it a few years ago." Andy asked, as they were taking five at the back door. Eric looked back without expression as though the concept of quitting was completely alien and unnecessary. With a shake of the head he replied.

"No."

Eric was one of those people that who didn't

appear to be moving that quickly, but he actually got a lot done. He was deceptively efficient. Andy *really* hoped he would stay on, at least in that part-time role. He lifted his spirit.

Day three was going so smoothly, Eric suggested that Andy would be fine on his own for the last hour, as he had an appointment he could do with keeping. Andy agreed, all he had to do was prepare the evening meal for the single patient they had and finish the last thirty minutes or so of service in the café, which he did without a hitch. He saw Dominic saunter in and out, with his entourage hanging on his every word. Dominic had still not called into the kitchen to see his new member of staff, which Andy found a bit *unusual.*

Just when Andy was finishing off and locking the fridges, a practice he thought a little strange… a place like the Haven that was supposedly dedicated to healing and giving, lacked the trust of human beings enough to risk leaving the fridges open overnight. Anyway, that's what they required, so that's what he would do. A voice called from the back door of the kitchen. It was John. *Oh no, here we go again,* thought Andy, the day had gone almost *too* smoothly up to that point.

"Could I borrow you for a moment?" John said, he held his right hand up and Andy could see that it was bleeding slightly, "Cut myself on a tile, do you have a plaster in the kitchen first aid box please?"

*That's a normal request.* "Sure wait a second." Andy said and then he went to the first aid box to get suitable plasters and something to wipe the blood away.

"You don't mind sorting it for me?" John asked.

"Of course not, no problem." Andy wiped the excess blood away and then selected from the first aid box, a size of plaster big enough to cover the wound. By the time he had opened the plaster wrapper and gone back to the wound....it had gone. Andy looked to see if he was mistaken, but he wasn't, there was no longer any need for the plaster. *Had John swapped hands whilst his back was turned?* He hadn't.

"I'm sorry I didn't mean to trick you. I took a chance you hadn't accidentally used it up for the day." John said.

Andy had a flashback to the other night, to Sally and her phantom cut in the bar.

"It's gone."

"Yes. Your touch can heal. I know it's hard to get your head around. I didn't believe it at first."

Andy said nothing for a few moments as he tried to assimilate the possibility that this guy was telling the truth and that he was not a kook after all. At last he said.

"I don't know what just happened." He was

not sure whether to believe his own eyes or not.

"It is a bit of a shock, I know." John said.

"This isn't possible." John did not look like a madman. There was compassion in his eyes, not madness, "This has to be a trick of some kind."

"I swear it's not a trick."

"It happened the other night, a girl cut herself on broken glass, then it disappeared…the cut."

"Did you touch her, skin to skin?" John asked. Andy nodded. John waited for the information that was overloading Andy's brain to settle in a little before he said anything else, "I could help demonstrate that this is real again, except for one small detail…you can only do it once per day."

"Once per day?"

"Yes, from dawn till dusk."

"Why is that?"

"I'm really sorry but I can't answer that one. Unfortunately I didn't make up the rules. It doesn't make it any more believable does it."

"Where does this thing come from?"

"I'm sorry, I can't answer that either." Andy was not convinced yet that he hadn't just witnessed an elaborate trick…perhaps this guy was a magician. This once per day notion wasn't helping him to believe it, "But I passed this ability on to you." John said.

"What do you mean you *passed it on*?"

"I had the power, now you have it."

"So, how could you do that and why pick me?"

"The day you started, actually before that, at the interview, I saw a light around you. Just like the person who passed it on to me said that I would. I passed it on when we shook hands that first day."

"So tell me why didn't you ask me first if I wanted this thing, *before* you passed it on?"

"I know, maybe I should have, but in a way I just knew it was the right moment and the right person."

Andy thought back to when he felt a jolt of what he thought was static when John had shaken his hand on that first day. It was starting to make sense, as incredulous as it appeared.

"Are you seriously telling me I can heal cuts just by touching the person?"

"Not just cuts...*anything.*"

"This just isn't possible."

"No, it isn't. But it happens."

"So if you had this, why pass it on?"

"I knew my time with it was up."

"How did you know?"

"I just knew. Also, I am retiring in a month."

"What would retiring have to do with it?"

"I wouldn't be in a position to use the gift so easily. That is the main reason why I started here: there are sick people. The other thing is, when I retire, I want to relax a little. The healing is a responsibility."

"Which you have now passed on to me."

"I know." John smiled, knowing he had also placed a particular burden on Andy's shoulders, "But I know I made the right choice."

"What am I supposed to do with this *gift*?"

"That is up to you, no one can tell you exactly what to do with it. That is what my mentor told me back when I got it."

"I have to heal one person per day." Andy stated.

"You don't *have* to. It took me a long time to realise this. The thing I would stress is, as long as you have the right *intentions*, if you have the *desire* to help, then you will...that is all you can do. Just abide by that principle and it will be ok." Andy looked a little shell shocked, all the trouble with Jane and now this coming out of left field, "I'm sorry if right now you resent me giving you this."

"I'm about to go home."

"I will be here tomorrow if you have more questions. No doubt you will. By the way, whilst you have this gift, you will never get ill, if it's been passed on the right way and I'm sure it has."

Andy half smiled, half frowned and then left. This was a real game changer in his thoughts and had planted itself front and centre stage, for now at least. The drive home was on auto-pilot.

# 14

*Never get ill.* Those three words reverberated around in Andy's head until he finally drifted off to sleep. He had wanted the Haven to be a fresh start and it was, but this was way off the scale. *What the hell was going on?* Perhaps when he woke up, the world would be back to normal, but then that was what he had been wishing for the last few months. People got sick of each other, grew apart, had affairs and split up every day, what had happened in his family life was painful, but *normal*, but this *gift* thing was a little more rarefied. That's if it wasn't just an elaborate trick pulled on a new member of staff. Sure he knew about sending the rookie for a glass hammer or a long stand on his first day at work, but this would have been on another level. Also, it had happened twice; the first time, when he was on the date. John was not around then. He drifted off into strange, unremembered dreams.

He woke not long after dawn. According to John, in the conversation they'd had the previous day which, for once, he seemed to remember every single word of; a new day and a new chance to heal one person. *One* person. *Why only one? What kind of crap was this?* No, he wasn't convinced; he needed more proof before he was even halfway to believing this absurd story.

He got dressed, drank a strong coffee and then another, as though the extra caffeine might snap him out of this dream-like trance that he found himself in. He tried to concentrate on the breakfast news, but found that he could not stop replaying the previous day with John's disappearing cut and also the evening with Sally, the drops of blood on the table and the unblemished smoothness of her hand.

He thought about how, since starting at the Haven, his messed up life had been turned on its head. Was that place jinxed? Was there some kind of voodoo spell on it? He needed to know for sure about the healing thing and he would find that out today, one way or another. Jane moving was a massive problem, but that could wait on hold for today at least. Today he would try the magic healing trick again and then this nonsense could be put to bed and he could get back to worrying about the stuff he was before, only with better shifts.

◆ ◆ ◆

Day four at the Haven. Andy slipped straight into a routine which began by starting the process of making the bread: mixing the yeast with the flour and water, then placing it somewhere warm and waiting for the yeast to weave its magic. He weighed the ingredients and mixed methodically, whilst pondering on what an ancient process this was. Jesus had broken bread and it had been a staple food for thousands of years. *Who first thought of doing this?* He wondered, as he formed the bread in to roll shapes on the stainless steel surface.

Eric was not quite on his usual chirpy form. He was wheezing and seemed a little out of breath. Andy had noticed Eric's cough at the interview, but this morning he was showing the tell-tale signs of years of smoking. He had gone to the back door and was coughing fairly continuously. Andy went over to him.

"Are you alright?" he asked.

Eric held up a hand as though to convey he would talk to Andy in a moment when he got his breath back. He was propping himself up with the other hand on the wall. Instinctively, with the desire to help, Andy steadied his hand on Eric's for a moment. Then all of a sudden, Eric coughed up something into the grass. The coughing stopped....didn't ease off or slow down, it just stopped. Eric levelled himself up.

"I needed to cough that up." he said, in a

clear and effortless voice. He didn't cough again for the rest of the day and Andy started to really believe what John had said was true: that he could heal people, and not just cuts. This was the third occasion it had happened and three strikes and you were out.

Andy looked for John at the end of the shift. He was mopping a corridor floor with a practiced rhythm when Andy tapped him on the shoulder. John switched off the Pink Floyd playing through his headphones.

"Ok, I get it." Andy said.

"Good, I knew you would…sooner or later."

"So, how do I go about this? What if I hand over some money at the garage and touch someone's hand, does that mean they are cured of something?"

"No, well sometimes it happens like that but most of the time you have to have the desire to help the person. The healing comes from that *intention*. But try not to over think it; you are not supposed to save everyone….you can't anyway."

"But how do I know *who* to help?"

"Follow your instincts. If a day goes by and you haven't healed anyone, then that's ok too. Again, it took me a while to get that."

"And if I don't want this?"

"You can pass it on also, at the right time and to the right person."

"How would I do that?"

"So many questions...I was just the same. You do what I did with you, make a *complete* circuit. Place both hands on the person's hand you wish to pass it on to and wish or desire the power to be transferred. It has to be the right person and the right intention."

"You said you saw a light around me?"

"Yes I did. Everyone has an aura, a certain vibration. You should be able to see this more clearly now you have the gift. Some of the more *developed* souls have a golden haze around them."

"Souls? Does it work in reverse; do bad people have a dark haze around them?"

"I've never really seen a dark haze it terms of colour, but it is different and I do sense a person's low vibration, which is similar. We all operate on electricity; the vibration is part of that. Certain emotions also vibrate at different speeds." John noticed that Andy was a little overwhelmed, once again, by all this new information. "Give it some thought, but don't rush into anything just yet, give it a little time. I'm sorry if you really don't want this, but it felt like I had no choice but to pass it on to you. It is difficult for me to explain why that was."

Andy nodded and walked slowly away. John watched him walk for a while; he remembered the day the gift was passed onto him. It came back clearer than it ever had done; the face of *his* mentor, Peter, as clear as day. He still spoke to Peter, now and then, on the phone, though not as often as he used to do. Peter was in his mid eighties now and had Alzheimer's; clarity of thought came and went when it felt like it and was one of the few things that the healing power hadn't worked on; possibly because it was not present the whole time. Or perhaps a former gift host could not be cured after they had passed it on.

Peter had kept the gift for twenty years, exactly the length of time John had said to himself he would keep it, right at the beginning. Peter had seen John, a quiet man, on his first day at work at the hospital he worked at and had seen the bright aura around him. He waited until he had gotten to know him a little better, after a few conversations in the canteen, and then decided he was *the one*. Peter had seen other people with an aura in the previous twenty years, but none had been brighter than John's. He had taken it as the right sign at the right time; he didn't really want to hang on to the gift after his self-imposed twenty years was up.

John had taken the explanation from Peter of what had happened in his stride, not exactly like it was the most natural thing in the world, but he was immediately more open to believing such things existed than Andy had appeared to be.

Peter and John had remained friends ever since. John sometimes wondered whether or not

Peter would have gone on to develop Alzheimer's, if he had kept the gift. Probably not. Anyway, they would never know, although it distressed John when he called Peter and he was largely incoherent on the other end. The worst thing was that he could do nothing at all about it; he *had* tried to on more than one occasion. If anyone had deserved healing it was Peter, after all the good he had done for others. It didn't seem fair, but then all the other people out there that needing healing probably felt the same way.

◆ ◆ ◆

The day went fairly smoothly. Andy could see the expensive cars coming and going through the kitchen window; Dom's white Range Rover being one of them. *This, really, was an exclusive playground for the rich.*

*All organic cafe.* Organic food really was something that those huge amounts of people out there on a very tight budget couldn't consider as an option. Andy himself only bought organic produce from the supermarket if it had been reduced and was on it's last day: as a chef he knew that vegetables had their *own* use-by date.

A couple of fifty something ladies popped their head in to the kitchen to meet and greet the new chef. They were pleasant enough and obviously well educated and rich. They were typical of people that watched *Masterchef* type programmes and saturday morning cookery shows. Andy felt like something of a celebrity, for a short time at least; albeit a low paid one.

When service was all finished, Andy sat in the office, ordering supplies on the computer. The woman that did the Haven's accounts, Carol, was also in the office working on the other computer. She seemed a little alien to the Haven and not part of the *theme*. For one, she wasn't wearing the off white unofficial/standard uniform that everyone else wore. She hadn't bought into the Haven's principles it seemed. A rebel. She came in once a week for two or three hours, crunched the numbers and then left. Not ever staying long enough to get drawn into the place's *vibe*. It paid well, but she had many similar positions.

"How are you settling in?" Carol asked.

Andy was half tempted to say quite well, apart from the mind blowing experience he'd had a couple of days ago, instead he said.

"Ok thanks."

"Have you met Dominic yet?"

"Er...no, he hasn't been in to see me yet."

"Does not surprise me."

"Oh, why not?"

Carol whispered. "He's a little up himself."

"Oh."

"Actually...more than a little. You will see him wandering around the place with his little band of hangers on."

Andy laughed. "I've already seen that, I thought it was Mick Jagger at first."

Carol seemed ok. Down to earth in a place with more than its fair share of people that weren't. She was an attractive woman in her early forties; she gave Andy the impression that she'd been there, seen it, done it and got the t-shirt to prove. She appeared a little a *hippy like*....a *maverick accountant*, two words he never thought would go together. She breezed in and out of several companies she looked after the accounts for, never getting personally attached to any of them.

From the office window there was a good view of the Haven's car park, which was still full of the gleaming chrome of premium brand vehicles, including Carol's five year old Mercedes.

"My advice would be, don't take anything here too seriously. Look at the cars out there." she continued, "The majority of people coming here think they can *buy* spirituality. A lot of them are bored rich housewives."

Andy looked up from the computer screen and concluded there may be a lot of truth in what she was saying. He did seem to have increased insight lately.

"What do you do if you have *so* much money; must get boring." Andy said, "Nice problem to have though." Andy hadn't been at the Haven for long and so he probably shouldn't have said much about his new employer, so he was a little bit guarded, after all he had only just met Carol, but he *kn*ew she was trustable. He could read people more clearly since acquiring the gift. He could see a faint glow around her, *or was that just the sunlight*? That was new as well. "Have you been here long?" he asked.

"Right from the start."

"It's an interesting place, no doubt. Though to be brutally honest; it was the hours that attracted me."

"Did you work nights at your previous job? A lot of chefs work nights don't they?"

"Yes, days and nights."

"Must be tough that."

"It can be. It's crap to be honest." Andy logged out of the computer. He'd been given his own log-in password, just to make him feel more at home. He told Carol it was nice to have met her, an idea which she reciprocated. That was him done for the day and he still felt like he was getting away with something.

The drive home again was like a journey between two realms; once he had passed the canopy of trees in the Haven's grounds, it was like a switch as though passing through a magic wardrobe back into the realm of normality, *in whatever that book was called*. This time, however, he knew for sure that he was carrying a gift along with him. Something he didn't ask for...straight out of a fairy tale.

# 15

The next day Andy awoke before the alarm went off. He had, not just a day in front of him, but what felt like an eternity. It was a whole different world, as though someone had given him a magic pill...*this is the world as it really is, it's not quite what you thought it was.* It wasn't exactly *Matrix-like,* but he was now aware of layers to life that not many other people knew about.

When he looked out of his window at the trees across the way, he saw them and indeed the whole of nature differently. Everything *was* connected, if it wasn't then this power he had wouldn't or couldn't exist. In fact, the whole universe seemed to him now to be one single unit; it wasn't just looking up at the stars the sun and moon and thinking *they look cool*; he felt very strongly that it was all one giant entity and that he was a part of it. So was everyone and everything else and there must've been so many things beyond what the average human being could comprehend or was aware of. John had not spoken about the awareness of him being a speck in the great scheme of things, it came over him all at once before fading into the background as the daily routine kicked in.

At the Haven, Eric was there to meet him. He told Andy how good he felt since coughing up whatever it was the day before. Andy smiled. He wasn't going to say "*Well actually, guess what....*" Although, he was not entirely sure whether this ability had to be kept secret or not, he did suppose it would be best if he did. Perhaps people would think he had lost the plot if he told anyone: after all, it had taken him three signs of proof to believe it himself. But it felt amazingly satisfying to have helped a person like Eric. Before service started, Eric still went for one of his French cigarettes, but this time he was starting with a clean slate.

Just before 12:00, Susan came into the kitchen with some paperwork. "We have two new patients arriving today." she said, passing the papers to Eric and Andy.,"Ian and Lucinda. These are their special dietary requirements plus any food allergies, likes and dislikes and anything else you need to know." She directed this mainly to Andy as, obviously, Eric knew the routine. Very often, in-patients would come down to the café to have their lunch and be given priority treatment, just to get them out of their rooms for a while. Often they were taken on walks through the grounds, before or afterwards or both, depending on their condition. The paperwork also gave a description of their illness. Whilst rarely a full house, the Haven had a steadily increasing stream of in-patients: word was getting out as the Haven's success stories racked up. You would still have to be of a certain mindset to consider the alternative healing methods, although some patients had exhausted all other possible forms of treatment, as Ian had. The slot on the local tv tea-time news was probably going to increase intakes once again; how much so was yet to be seen.

Andy studied the papers with Eric who explained that they got these papers as a matter of routine every time they had someone new in for treatment. Rather than looking first at the dietary requirements, as would have been expected, Andy looked at their treatment plan and illnesses. John had told him not to feel like he had to heal someone *every* day, and even if he did, it didn't necessarily have to be someone at the Haven. Andy got a mental picture of Ian and Lucinda in his head and felt compelled to make a choice.

Linda had back pain which was acute. Something that an operation may or may not have been able to fix; but with a chronic fear of surgery, she was trying the Haven's methods first. Usually it was the other way around.

Ian had been suffering with severe migraine headaches. He had been thoroughly checked out, including C.A.T scans, and there were no obvious abnormalities; the doctors could find no medical reason whatsoever for the migraines; all they could do was prescribe pain killers which Ian had felt progressively and uneasily accustomed to. He had heard about the Haven through a mutual friend and was willing to give its methods *a go*.

*Neither life threatening, no obvious choice,* thought Andy. So what should he do? Toss a coin? *Heads Ian and tails Lucinda.* Was he supposed to use the gift to heal anything *less* than life threatening? He was still, understandably, trying to figure all this out. If it *was* the case that he should only heal seriously ill people, then he would be better suited in a hospital; although it would not have been as easy to access patients on the critical wards, if at all...unless he spent around eight years training to become a doctor. If he was a paramedic, he pondered, that would be ideal...except then what would he do? Heal the first critical patient he came across? What if there was someone else more in need later in the day, or a child just starting out in life? The guilt and regret would be overwhelming. John had come to terms with the role he had played and he was going to have to do the same. He came up with an idea that may help him to heal more easily; he asked Susan.

"Do the chefs ever go out and chat to the patients? Get some feedback? I think that would be a nice *touch*."

"Well they haven't done so far, but I agree, if you would like to do that it's a good idea." Susan replied.

"I mean, not every time obviously, but every now and then." Andy said.

"Great. Keep a nice clean apron on standby." Susan joked, after looking at Andy's apron covered in flour and other unidentifiable things, "Ian is on a particular diet, *very specifically* no nuts; it's all there on the sheet anyway." Susan added before she left.

Andy could not decide who to heal first. So it's going to be whoever he saw first, he thought. He was eager to try the gift out again, as the other one's *may* possibly have just been a fluke. He also wanted to try it out on other illnesses.

The first patient that he saw was Ian, he was in the café at lunchtime. He ordered soup and a sandwhich. Andy went over to the table with the pretence of asking whether or not he enjoyed lunch and he found an easy enough way to make brief skin contact, whilst having the intention to help and heal in his mind. *Clear your mind and wish for healing to take place, even for just a second or two*, John had said.

Ian seemed like a decent man. He smiled and thanked Andy, told him that the soup was really nice. Later he went through the treatment sessions with both the crystal and the electromagnetic machines. When, after the third day of treatments had passed and he reported no more headaches, all involved assumed it was down to the Haven's magical machines.

Andy was left in no doubt after this. He did manage to repeat the trick with Lucinda on the next day and cure her of her back trouble. Of course no one except John knew for sure that it wasn't the alternative treatments that were responsible for these two minor miracles. In fact, no one picked up on the fact that Lucinda's slight arthritis had also gone away for good, or that Ian's cold had disappeared at the same time as his headaches. In a way, the Haven was actually like some kind of modern day wild-west medicine show; *cure all ills*, thought Andy, with Dominic perfectly cast as the unscrupulous hawker.

# 16

The highlight of the week for Andy was the day he picked the kids up from school. Things went back, for a time at least, to a piece of normality; especially after recent events. But this occasion was different. As he took his place in the school playground, ready to greet Fran and Jack when the bell sounded, he spotted someone. Standing, waiting in a red dress stood Jane, talking to another kid's mother, smiling and joking. She spotted Andy from out of the corner of her eye, said *bye* to the other mum and then dropped the smile from her mouth like a sack of potatoes. She walked over to him with arms folded. Andy said nothing, but waited for her to speak. She'd never done this since they had split.

"Are you ok?" Jane asked. She got no reply. Andy studied her with suspicion, lately her actions had done nothing but cause him damage, and greeting her would be like shaking the executioner's hand just moments before he chopped your head off, "It's definite now; we are moving." she continued, with arms still folded, "In four weeks."

*Why had she come to the playground to tell him this?* Probably so that he couldn't cause a major scene that would paint him as *the bad one*. Most of the other parents had heard about recent events: it's a small school. Some had no interest, some had heard Andy walked out on them and thought him an asshole, some knew of the affair and thought Jane was at fault. Andy had said nothing to the other parents as he didn't want the fallout to negatively impact on the kids.

"You can't do that." he said.

"I can. I'm sorry, but that is what is happening."

If she was sorry, it didn't manifest on her face or indeed in the aura that Andy could now read more clearly.

"It's too far."

"You will still get to see the kids, just not as often."

"You are going 200 miles away; that's hardly a round trip."

"We will sort out a schedule, but we *are* moving. I'm sorry, but it's not something you can stop. I don't think it would be a good idea to fight it."

Andy knew she was probably right. There was no way he would win a custody battle, the man rarely did, and he also knew that this *new* version of Jane would throw up or make up anything to smear him... like he smoked weed in the past, for example, and he also had no doubt she would just fabricate all else that she needed. Also, he only had the small flat and needed to hold down a job, so would not be able to spend enough time with the children. The deck was brutally stacked against him. Andy wanted to plead with her, appeal to her good nature, but he knew it would have no effect and the way she had been acting lately suggested she would enjoy watching him grovel. Her feet were shifting stance and his felt heavy and rooted to the ground. Anger and the flight or fight response gripped him. He resisted lashing out, though he pictured it in his mind, or doing something he might regret later. *Maybe that was what she wanted.*

The bell rang and the doors of the school opened; children came pouring out to their mums and dads. Fran came out and stopped for a second when she saw both parents standing there. She made a bee line for Andy and stood next to him, a little bewildered as to why both parents were there, like they used to be. *Were they now friends again?* She did hope so; she could have dad around all the time. Rick was alright, but he wasn't dad. She looked at each of them in turn for some kind of clarification.

In the background, a black BMW pulled over and Jane saw that Rick had arrived to collect her.

"I've already spoken to the kids." Jane said, before walking away.

"What did mum want?" Fran asked.

"I'll tell you a bit later."

"Do we have to move still?"

Obviously it had been discussed at home. Jack came out and joined them.

"I think so Fran." Andy said.

"We are moving Jack." Fran said. Jack's face dropped.

"Can't we stay here with you? Can't you go to the Judge?" Jack asked.

"I don't think the Judge will allow it."

"I will speak to the Judge." Jack said.

"I don't think he would listen."

"Aren't Judges supposed to listen to everyone and then do the right thing?" Jack asked.

"Yes they are, but, I only have a small flat and they usually decide children should stop with their mum." In the background, the black BMW revved and zipped off with a squeal of tyres, "Don't you want to try another town? It might be exciting." Andy asked them both.

"No we don't. Fran thinks the same as me. Mum says we have to start calling Rick *dad* after we move. But I'm not going to." Jack said.

"Not me either." Fran agreed.

Feeling like his heart could explode, Andy led his kids to his car. They got in and then he steadily drove off. It started to rain and one of the windscreen wipers decided to break, leaving Andy a smaller window to see out of on the way home.

◆ ◆ ◆

The night with the kids had a cloud hanging over it as sure and ominous as the clouds that were providing the rain. That thing that nobody wanted was off in the distance, but everyday it was edging nearer, seemingly unavoidable like a storm that had been predicted to hit town. They did the usual: eat, play games, watch a bit of tv. The drive to drop them back off the next day was done mainly in silence; none of the three cracked a smile. This time Jane was not at home. It was Rick standing in the doorway.

"Mum said she might be late." Jack said.

The two kids got gingerly out of the car and headed on in. Andy knew he had no choice but to just let them go in. Rick gave them each a pat on the head as they went in. He gave Andy a false smile and had a smug aura about him. It was an unpleasant colour. When the kids had gone inside, Andy said.

"Proud of yourself are you?" Rick did not reply, unaffected, it seemed. "Splitting up a family?" Andy continued, "You're fine with that?"

"That's just the way it goes." Rick replied.

"Is that all you can say?"

"There are winners and losers in every game."

"Just a game to you is it?"

The kids were watching through the window.

"My advice is to move on; this is just the way it is. No hard feelings."

"The move, is that your idea?"

"Might be."

"Well is it or not?"

"Could be."

At this point Jane pulled up and got out of her car.

"So it is for him that you are moving." Andy said to her. The kids were still watching.

"I never suggested otherwise." she replied. Rick's smug grin got a little broader; he was not even trying to conceal it. Andy had never really experienced real *hatred* before, but this guy standing at the door had stepped firmly into that category. The kids were watching still, so Andy had to curb his emotions as best he could, he didn't want them both traumatized as well as himself. Jane grabbed her new partners arm and they went inside, without organizing the next stay over. Andy was simply too angry to talk any more. He stood looking at the house for a few seconds, before getting back into his car.

For the rest of the day his thoughts were filled with those five minutes of time, replaying like a video clip stuck on rewind. He couldn't see a way out, not with Jane as robotic and emotionless as she was. What he needed was *another* miracle.

# 17

Whilst he was waiting for that next miracle to arrive, Andy did get something by way of a distraction. The next time he was in the office ordering supplies, Carol was also in there again and they began chatting as they had the previous week. She noticed that Andy looked troubled and asked him if everything was ok. Andy ended up giving her the shortened down version of events with regards to Jane and the kids and she showed genuine concern; which he knew was genuine because of his enhanced intuition.

"What you need is a distraction." she said, "Some chill out time." She then invited him around to her house the next evening for a drink. He was a little taken aback as he had only just met her, but they *had* hit it off straight away, and he thought it couldn't do any harm so he said yes, he would like to. She said she would make some food, but asked him in advance not to be too critical of it, with him being a chef. He agreed and for the life of him, he couldn't think of any reason why not; it wasn't strictly a date and she seemed to have a good outlook on life; her enthusiasm and positivity was contagious.

◆ ◆ ◆

The next day passed swiftly. There were no new patients but they did get the notification of two more arriving the next day. Andy was studying the information sheets with Eric, when suddenly Eric ripped the bottom off the sheet where it listed the patient's illness: the part they didn't really need for their department. He'd forgotten his lighter and used the paper to get a light from the stove and then he lit a cigarette at the back door.

"You know." Eric said, "It almost feels like I've never smoked for most of my life."

Andy tried to make out the treatment schedule for the new patient. It was the crystal machine and also something else that had been ripped away. He supposed it didn't matter, as whatever it was they had it would be gone in a few days if all went according to plan. He would try and make contact with this patient, Catherine, first. The other patient was seventy eight year old Gerald. He had a hip problem and was in for physio and faith healing. *Surely a winning combination.*

"What exactly is the faith healing all about?"

Andy asked Eric.

"Oh that. They lie them down on a table, put their hands on them and chant. It's a load of bollocks if you ask me." replied Eric.

"Who does that?"

"All of them that think they can heal. Dom is one of them. That man is a bigger ego-maniac than Bonaparte."

"Does it ever work?"

"Not that I am aware of."

This made Andy think. If he, *or when he,* healed Gerald, all those self proclaimed faith healers would think that they had something. *Would it be wrong to allow them that?* Then he remembered John's words, *don't over think it.* He repeated that line to himself a few times.

"So what do you think Eric, are you going to stay on?" He asked, knowing that he was now able to run the kitchen on his own.

"I don't know. I might do. It is better now that you are here, the pressure is off me, plus, I seem to have more energy these last few days...quite a lot more for some reason. Maybe you are a good luck charm." he added, with the hint of French accent. He followed that up with a slightly in tune rendition of the 80's punk song *Ca plane pour moi.*

◆ ◆ ◆

Work was routine and fairly uneventful. It

was almost *too* easy. At one point during the day, Andy saw Dom on the car park having a heated discussion with someone who looked pretty brow-beaten. Behind Dom was one of the shaven headed gorillas from earlier, who looked about as friendly as a lion with toothache.

Soon it would be time to meet up with Carol. *It's not strictly a date as such,* he reminded himself, and anyway, he'd had one of those recently and it went ok, so there was no need to feel nervous at all.

She lived on a street he'd never been to before, with nice detached houses; they weren't massive mansions, but they were in comparison to his little flat. *Perhaps he should have tried harder in maths lessons. Carol must be comfortably off.* The door bell chimed a sophisticated little tune and she answered the door, dressed less smartly than when at work, but in a classy kind of casual style. She looked good; exactly right. Andy hadn't asked her age of course as, out of practice as he was, he knew that you're not supposed to; that was one golden rule he hadn't forgotten. Mind, the last time he had asked that, the girl in question, Jane, was still only a teenager. She invited him in, took his jacket and asked him how ready he was for dinner.

"Oh, you really didn't need to go to much trouble." he said. Looking around, but trying not to appear like he was looking around, "But whenever really, I skipped tea."

She beckoned for him to sit at the table whilst she made the finishing touches to dinner.

"Do you want some wine?" she asked. Andy replied that he would be ok with one glass as he was driving. She poured him a glass of white, he didn't really drink white often, but it was going to compliment the food later. It was in the £10-£15 pound bracket of wine; an area of the supermarket shelf that he never really ventured into...unless it was on special offer. He took a sip; it tasted better than any other wine he had tasted, white or red. A lot smoother than the £5 stuff he normally got. Before long, Carol appeared with two plates of steaming food and she placed them down on the nicely set up, but not *too* fancy table.

"Hope you like Paella." she said.

"Yeah sure, looks great."

It was perfectly done with succulent king prawns on top. Not overcooked, which was the common mistake with this dish.

"It's excellent." Andy commented, after just one forkfull.

"Thanks. My Gran used to make this, she taught me how."

"Was she Spanish?" Andy joked.

"Yes she was."

That explained the authenticity of the dish and it also explained why she was so dark haired and olive skinned.

"You do have the Mediterranean complexion." he said. She smiled. She did know that, but it was nice that he seemed to appreciate it. The conversation flowed nicely; not hurried or forced in any way. After a while she said.

"Tell me more about your kids."

Andy appreciated her interest. He gave her the *concise* version of the last year or so; not being one of those parents that think others want to hear every last detail about someone else's children. He also told her about the moving situation. Then he asked Carol if she had any children. She told him about her one son in his early twenties, who apparently spent his time driving around in a VW camper, smoking weed and surfing; though not at the same time.

"Sounds idyllic." Andy said.

"He can't do it forever...though I don't suppose he'll want to." she commented, "Hopefully not anyway."

Andy found himself laughing during the conversation; something he hadn't done for a while. By the time Carol brought out dessert, a Tiramisu, he had finished the glass of wine he had allocated himself.

"Do you want a top up?" she asked.

"Thanks, but I better not drive on any more."

"If you want another glass, you can always stay over, I have a spare bed."

Andy did want another glass, but did he want

to stay over? He took a few seconds to decide.

"Are you sure that's ok?"

"Sure."

"Ok then, you have convinced me."

Carol refilled his glass. It really was nice wine and was helping him start to relax. This lady was charming, even her voice was soothing; the complete opposite of Jane in her present state. She chatted to Andy briefly about her ex husband, and how they had a villa in Spain. They used to rent a boat for months at a time and travel around the coast. They had split on good terms and remained friends. *A real rarity*. The conversation switched back and forth effortlessly for the next couple of hours. Carol asked what time he was at work the next day, he replied seven am, but reassured her not to worry as he could manage alright on four hours sleep. Carol offered him a nightcap, she poured cognac into nice glasses, not huge measures but just the right amount; they sipped them and chatted some more, the warmth of the brandy echoed the warmth from Carol. The wooden clock in the hallway chimed: it was midnight. She showed him upstairs to the spare room, then she disappeared briefly into her own room before coming back to stand in the doorway, having changed into nightwear.

"It's up to you where you want to sleep." she said quietly, after a subtle pause. Andy had taken off his shirt, not really expecting her to re-appear.

He was not sure he wanted any complications, but the wine and brandy had blurred the edges. Carol's long dark hair was flowing down over her feminine shoulders. He took a step towards her in the corridor. They kissed gently. He placed his hand on her waist and closed her bedroom door behind them.

Andy woke first the next day at six am; he left Carol still sleeping and got dressed in the spare room. He managed to find some paper and left her a note*, Thanks for a great evening, Andy X.* He left the house with a glowing feeling of being wanted, for a night at least. The day ahead was gilded with a hint of optimism.

# 18

It was the day of the broadcast of the local news feature on the Haven, scheduled to be on the tea-time slot. Dom had gathered some select friends at his large, white detached house that bordered on mansion proportions.

Dom's wife, Felicity, had been in awe of him ever since she had heard him speak to her about her anxiety issues. In truth, she lacked the grounded state of mind needed to make a rational assessment of him. She was exactly his type of play-thing: an unconditional admirer. She drifted through life as though medicated or stoned, without actually being so.

Dom had never cheated on her, that wasn't his thing. He got just as much pleasure from knowing he had the option to cheat on her if he wanted to, and that she was so far under his control that she would never discover anything he'd done. She was there to give him emotional stability, a slow drip feed of supply, and also, to make him look, from the outside, like any other *normal* person.

Did he love her? Not in the normal sense of the word, the same as he hadn't ever loved anyone else either. When his Grandfather had passed away when he was ten years old, his first thought had been *could I now get to sit in his comfortable chair?*

Two other couples had been given the privilege of joining them. Alex and Christina were both psychotherapists and also both very similar in personality to each other. They lived *their* dream of both control and extreme wealth and were also similarly dressed to Dom in white and pastel coloured cotton suits, organic of course. Actually, they looked like extras from a 1980's *Miami Vice* episode. The second couple were Mike and Bob, both dentists. Mike was Felicity's brother. They wore expensive, but plainer, darker coloured clothes and had the slightly sadistic look that dentists often carried with them outside of surgery hours.

Felicity had made some nibbles and she had opened a bottle of bubbly. They sat chatting in front of the large hi-tech tv screen. The feature, filmed the previous week, was due to screen at 5:45 and Dom had already started recording the show, just in case it came on early.

The conversation was generally pretty light-hearted between these friends; rarely did they venture into serious subjects and, to be honest, rarely did they say anything of much significance.

But, it felt re-affirming to all present to be surrounded by people of similar wealth. The sweet scent of success filled the room.

Dom shushed the chatter and turned up the volume when the presenter cued up the feature on the Haven. Felicity clapped her hands excitedly. The programme host gave a little background information on the Haven, before the camera cut to Dom himself; wearing the most highly polished version of his metaphorical mask.

"You look classy." said Bob.

"Very handsome." said Christina.

Dom was answering all the questions from the presenter with an assured calmness, and playing his part to perfection. This kind of attention was what he had always dreamed of. No one would have cared enough to interview Dominic the property tycoon, or given him a feature on television, but Dominic the *healer*...Dominic the almost *guru*-like figure was now getting the appreciation he rightly deserved.

Then, after a few minutes of screen time, his masterfully played scene was over and the feature cut to the inside of the Haven and a view of some of the machines. This is where things went a bit *off*. The tone of the voice commentating had started off serious, but now it seemed to be a little insincere....mocking almost. As the reporter described in more detail what the Haven was all about, there was more than a hint of sarcasm creeping in to her tone of voice with each passing moment.

"The Haven *claims* that these machines and other techniques can fix any ailment known to man." Indeed, the commentary was now making the Haven seem like a modern day version of an old western medicine show. *Why hadn't they told him they were going to take this angle and make it a joke!* Dom was silently seething. After one last parting shot from the presenter, that was it, the few minutes were over and the story on the Haven came across as one of those funny stories that they tag on at the end of the news to make you laugh: the funny cat story or quadruplets in Canada. Dom's small gathered entourage fidgeted awkwardly in their seats.

Reeling from the humiliation, Dom clicked the recording off, and then switched the tv off completely. He was hoping for and expecting more adoration, but had ended up looking like a clown, complete with white suit. All he'd needed to complete the look were the oversized shoes and a red nose. His companions were kind of thinking the same, except for Felicity who thought it all went perfectly fine.

"That was alright." Alex said.

"Started off really well." Bob said.

"Any publicity is good publicity." Mike said.

It was attention and reactions that Dom

wanted; he preferred good feedback but bad reactions were fine too, they worked for him as well, but not this....not humilated on television for the entire world to see. His false sense of self was reeling. *I'll show them; I'll bury this with more and more results. Then they will have to get down on their knees and apologise to me for this. I'll get her sacked. She'll never work again. It's time I went to see John the cleaner....make him a proposition he won't refuse.*

# 19

Sean tapped on the steering wheel as he waited. Patience was not one of his virtues. Then, he saw a light go out in a third floor office in the block he was watching. That meant his target was on the move. He left his vehicle and pulled the hood of his black jacket over his head as he slowly and calmly walked down to the car park underneath the office block. There was just one CCTV camera pointing in the direction he didn't want; he skilfully tossed a cover over it as he strolled past. There were only three cars left in the car park; it was the Jaguar he was interested in. He waited a few moments until it's sidelights flashed and the patter of expensive shoes echoed and reverberated around the enclosed space. Then Sean spoke. "Excuse me." The briefcase carrying figure stopped and turned to see Sean's large frame silhouetted by the car park's lights.

"Can I help you?"

"Yes I think maybe you can. Mr Rollins isn't it?"

Rollins did not want to confirm or deny; his gut was telling him to be cautious. Sean wanted to confirm he had the right man; a few months previously he had made an error. A grey Jaguar, Dom had said; this had to be the right guy. He walked over with a blank expression like he was strolling over to the office water dispenser, and he landed two heavy punches to the body of the man, making him double over in pain. A blow to the back of the head sent him sprawling to the ground. Rollins wanted to offer money to this assailant to stop the assault, but was too badly hurt to speak. A kick in the ribs made Rollins curl up into a fetal position and he lay there, motionless. Sean picked up his briefcase and opened the Jaguar door. There wasn't much worth taking, but it was surprisingly untidy inside, for a well-heeled mark like this one. He rooted around but found nothing much. The guy on the floor was moving a little. Sean took a quick look around and then casually walked back to the entrance, where he pulled the cover off the camera as he walked past out of its range of vision. He slowly walked away, climbed back in to his car and then cruised onwards.

Ten minutes later, his car pulled up next to a Range Rover on a leafy suburban street. Sean said nothing as he passed the briefcase through the window. "It's done?" The voice from the white car asked.

"Yeah."

"You weren't followed?"

"Nope."

"You changed the plates?"

"Yep." A hand passed a paper bag containing notes from the white car to Sean's, who took a quick look, but did not bother to count it, "You sure there's no CCTV round here?"

"Do you think that I'd be here if there were. Well done, once again. By the way, he's not dead is he?"

"Na, I don't think so. He's got the message though and you got the breifcase."

The Range Rover pulled away. Sean didn't bother asking what was in the briefcase or who Rollins was; it was none of his business. He'd made it look like a simple mugging as requested.

When he arrived back at his lock-up, he placed the bag of money on the table. Not a bad night's work, if you worked it out at an hourly rate; particularly so as it was a one man job and he wasn't splitting the money. He lined up some powder on the coffee table and poured himself a Jack Daniels.

◆ ◆ ◆

Three weeks until the move. Over recent days, Andy had developed a pleasantly surprising bond with Eric. It was of the sort that was quite rare.

First impressions can be a false reflection of a person's *soundness* when often, over time, the true personality of a person shines through and then you want to keep your distance. With Eric, it was the complete opposite. He only worked a few days now and they overlapped shifts only occasionally, but when they did, he had the effect of putting a smile on the face of Andy and anyone else that he encountered. He just had that effect on people by being himself. Sometimes he would make jokes about the French, his favourite lines were about their ineptitude when fighting wars. "*We have open-top submarines.*" But, no one else was allowed to diss the French in his company. A delivery driver had called him a *frog*, in jest. Eric showed no sign of amusement as he grabbed him by the scruff of the neck. "*I can call myself a frog....you can't...got that?*"

Andy had explained, as they were working, his situation with the kids, Jane, the boyfriend and the upcoming move. He wasn't guarded about anything with Eric, even though he had only known him a short time. "What is she trying to achieve?" Andy asked him.

"It sounds like." Eric responded, matter of factly, "She is punishing you."

"For what?"

"For what she is doing. Or, for what someone else has done."

"That makes no sense."

"In France we have a saying."

"What's that?"

"Women…make no sense…*roughly translated.* Once you accept that knowledge, life becomes a lot simpler. My father taught me that." He strolled over to the back door to light up, "Try not to over complicate anything; you will never work it out what is happening in some other people's minds. A lot of the time, you don't want to."

Andy wondered whether he would ever need to heal Eric again in the future, as clouds of cigarette smoke filled the air. His overall laid back attitude was what enabled Eric to take everything in his stride. It was solid wisdom in its own right, yet different to Ramesh's.

Later on in the day, Eric went on to tell Andy about his great, great, great Grandfather, who was a part of Napoleon's cannon crew at Waterloo. Andy had no idea whether or not any of his ancestors had been there that day, on Wellington's side or otherwise. In fact, he didn't know any details of any family history past the level of his grandparents. Eric found this unusual.

"Why not?" Eric asked.

"Dunno, just a general lack of interest. Maybe there are some skeletons in closets somewhere. My parents never mentioned much about family. They were too busy arguing."

"One day I'll tell you about my great aunt."

"What did she do?"

"She ran the biggest house of ill repute in Nice."

"Oh. *Nice* in Nice."

"Kept a lot of old soldiers happy....and a lot of young ones too probably."

"Perhaps I'll get around to doing a family tree someday."

"It's an eye opener. I found out about my lot....why do you think I moved to England." Eric said, without smiling. *Was he being serious?* You could never really tell. Andy laughed whether or not.

The job at the Haven was pretty good. Despite his other circumstances, Andy was enjoying it as much as he could do, under present circumstances. It occurred to him more strongly than ever, that it was the people you are with that make something good or bad or indifferent. Everything else can be incidental.

# 20

Eighteen days until the move, according to Jane's schedule, and the inevitability felt sickening. Andy was trying to put a brave face on, but he knew underneath that he was going to miss the children terribly. It felt like a runaway train that couldn't be stopped.

Fran seemed to be her usual chirpy self, when Andy greeted her in the playground. "We have a new girl in the class." she said, "Her birthday is next week."

"Oh, that's nice." Andy replied.

"But, she isn't so well. They sat her next to me. I think I heard the teacher say, because I am friendly."

"I'm sure that's right." Andy said, as they started to walk to Jack's part of the school. Fran turned and waved to the new girl, who was being guided out to her parents. She had an oxygen mask to help with her breathing, "What is wrong with her Fran?"

"Miss did say so, but I can't remember what

she said. It was a word I didn't know."

"Not to worry." Andy re-affirmed to himself that, despite the worries with Jane moving and all that was associated with that, he...*they* were still very lucky.

"But, I heard Billie and Ella saying they didn't want to make friends with her."

"Oh. Why's that?"

"I think it's because she has to have a mask on sometimes."

"To help her breathe?"

"I think so. And, she can't run either...in the playground. She's not allowed. She just had to sit down and watch."

"That's a shame."

"Why do some people have to be like that dad? Have they done something bad?"

"Bad?"

"You know, something they have done wrong, so then they have to wear a mask."

"No, no. It's just what happens sometimes, but it's not her fault."

"But why does it happen?"

"I'm not sure." Andy tried to think of a way to explain. He couldn't: there was no explanation.

"She has invited me to her house. It's her birthday on Saturday."

"That's nice. Is she having a party?"

"Yes, but mum can't take me; she is going somewhere with Rick."

In his mind, Andy replaced Rick with *prick*. "Oh. Do you want me to take you? If your mum is ok with that."

"Can you dad?"

"Sure." Andy did have plans, but hopefully nothing that couldn't be altered. Jack came out of his part of the school to join them. He looked like Andy: sad but trying to put a brave face on.

◆ ◆ ◆

The next day, he dropped the kids off at school in the morning and then had no other plans for the rest of the day. Eric was working at the Haven; Andy planned to ask him if he would do Saturday for him, so that he could take Fran to the new girl's party. He already knew, somehow, that he would say *yes* to the request.

When he got back to his flat, he sat next to the living room window, sipping coffee and watching the rain hit the glass. The droplets moved this way and that in the gusty wind. For some reason, he thought about Eric and his cigarettes. Andy had given up smoking five years previously. Now that he had *the never get ill* bonus that came with the gift, he could start again...if he wanted to. Perhaps they would help calm his agitated state. Then he remembered the astronomical cost of the things and consigned the idea of restarting to being one of the worst he'd ever had; alongside getting involved with Jane, though if he hadn't have done that, there would be no Jack or Fran. In a few weeks time, they would still be around...just a lot further away.

He watched the rain fall some more and then wondered what to do with the rest of the day; it felt very empty. Jane was collecting the kids from school, so his day now had no structure. He watched tv for a while, then played a game on the laptop. He did have a strong feeling of inertia and felt there was something else that he should be doing. The only way to remedy this was to go back to bed....*catch up on some sleep*, he said to himself. When he woke an hour later, the feeling had faded but it was still there. He realised that feeling at peace was one of the greatest commodities a human being can possess.

He got dressed and walked down to the supermarket, where he tried to fill the emptiness he felt, for a time at least. He walked down the alcohol aisle and studied the whiskeys. He didn't really want to get any and he felt like  if he did, he would be using it as a crutch. He compromised with a half bottle, before buyin a few other bits and peices and then setting off back to the flat. There were people he could have called in to see to talk to, but he wasn't in the mood. He sat, solitary, with a glass of whiskey in his hand, mulling things over. He watched the rain a little longer and then it dawned on him that he hadn't healed anyone that day; it had gotten to dusk before he'd even realised. He looked up at the darkening sky and felt the pull of regret about the wasted chance. John had told him that he had to always bear in mind that he was under no obligation to heal someone every day. But he *did* feel some obligation, but to who? God? Andy thought it would take a bit longer to come to terms with this notion. All he could do for now was take another sip of whiskey.

◆ ◆ ◆

On the way to the Haven the next morning, Andy made a pledge to himself that he would definitely use his gift before they day was out. It niggled at him that yesterday he hadn't. *Don't feel as though you have to use it.* He repeated John's words to himself as he pulled up in the newly designated *staff parking area.* Dom had decided it would be *applicable* for the staff to park their cars out of sight, around the back. It had nothing to do with, of course, his staff not being able to afford the BMW's, Audi's, Mercedes & Porsche's etc that his clients populated the main car park with. He wanted to maintain the ambiance and the not so subtle illusion of wealth and prosperity that permeated the whole operation. Andy's slightly rusting twelve year old Ford certainly did not fit the image.

"They should pay us more then." Eric had said about the staff parking area, "I'll drive around in a Porsche, no problem."

"Is that what you'd get, if money was no object?" Andy asked.

"No. German." Eric replied.

"Oh. Don't you like German stuff?"

"No, especially their tanks."

"Ah, world war two a sore point." Andy said, he still couldn't tell whether or not Eric was serious.

"If they had invaded England, you'd feel the same way."

"They didn't invade, just bombed the crap out of us."

"Yeah, true. You didn't want to live in Coventry….or London. No, I am joking about German cars; I would have one. Life is too short to bear grudges on people long since dead." Eric had ignored the staff parking rule and still parked his Renault wherever he saw a free space.

After lunch, Andy sat with John in the café and had a cup of organic coffee with him. John was still adapting to no longer having the gift. Every time he felt a twinge or coughed, it reminded him that he no longer had the *never get ill* bonus that came with the gift. "So." John asked, "How are you adapting?"

Andy exhaled. "I suppose as well as could be expected. I didn't heal anyone yesterday at all."

"You will have many days like that."

"It didn't feel right."

"I know exactly what you mean and what you are feeling. I was the same. I can remember as if it were yesterday."

"So it doesn't last, this feeling that I've let someone, somewhere down."

"No, it will fade in time, as most things do. You are going to do a lot of good; but you won't and can't every single day."

Andy nodded. In the background, Dom sauntered in to the café with Sue close behind.

"Does he always wear those white cotton clothes?" Andy asked John.

"Seems to. Probably has white cotton pyjamas as well."

"He still hasn't been in to say *hello* or *welcome* or anything."

"He is like that. He ignored me for a long time, and then all of a sudden, almost overnight, he started smiling and taking a big interest. Not that I was bothered. He seems to live in a fantasy world."

"Now, we both know that the fantasy world is a reality." Andy said, with a smile.

"It is. Only us select few know it. It's best to just leave them to whatever they do. He is a tricky one to read though. His aura is vague; at least that's what I got. What do you think?"

"I don't know. I haven't been too close to him.

It almost feels like there is something blocking me reading him properly."

"It's not an exact science."

"Yeah." Andy agreed. He felt better having spent some time with John; it had given him new focus and perspective on the whole situation. At the moment, he felt like he needed all the help he could get.

# 21

Two weeks until the move. Eric had agreed to cover the Saturday shift, so Andy was able to take Fran to the birthday party. He pulled up outside his old house just before 10:00 am. Jane didn't bother coming out at all, but Fran came out on her own carrying a little gift bag. She climbed into the car seat in the back of his car, not really smiling that much to say she was on the way to a party.

"Everything ok?" Andy asked her, as he clicked her seatbelt together.

"Yeah."

"Where's Jack?"

"He's in his room. He's always in his room." Fran said. They set off.

"Does he not come downstairs often?"

"No. He doesn't like Rick so much."

"Oh." Andy felt another jolt of pain. There was nothing he could do about that, "Anyway, are you looking forward to the party?"

"Yeah, I suppose."

"You don't sound too sure."

"It's ok."

Andy's Ford pulled up outside Natalia, the new girl's house. "This is it." Andy said. He didn't ask why her mother or even Rick could not have taken her. Fran looked towards the house and saw balloons and cards in the window. Andy got out and lifted Fran out of her car seat, before escorting her to the front door, where Natalia's mum was waiting to welcome her in. Andy smiled at the lady. "Have a great time." he said, before going back to the car. He thought about calling in to see Jack, he had a couple of hours free until he needed to pick Fran up again; it *would* mean having to speak to Jane, but he went anyway. When he got to the house, there was no one in and the car was gone. His heightened sense of empathy meant that he felt his son's suffering. Jack must've felt like an outsider in his own home. Andy hoped that Jane would put her own son's wellbeing first. This new version of Jane didn't seem to be doing that.

Feeling at a loose end and with a bit of time to kill, Andy drove to Mick's new place of work. He was relieved to see Mick's car on the car park. *No staff parking rules here.* Andy texted Mick, who came out to open the back door. He saw Andy just standing there, looking deep in thought.

"You ok pal?" Mick asked.

"Yeah, I suppose. I just had some time to kill before I pick Fran up."

"For a minute there I thought you just wanted to see your old buddy."

"Well maybe a little."

"How's the new job going?"

"It's ok." Andy jousted with the idea of telling Mick more.

"What about that weird guy?"

"Oh.....he's turned out to be ok. What's it like here?"

"Good." Mick said, and then he disappeared back into the kitchen for a while. He returned with a coffee for Andy, who he'd figured needed a bit of *pepping up*. Andy took a drink.

"What's in here?" Andy asked.

"Just a shot of cooking brandy. It's a liqueur coffee."

"I'm driving."

"The coffee will sober you up. You heard any more from Sally?"

"Nope."

"Probably just as well. Like I said, just practice."

"Yeah."

Mick briefly thought about telling Andy about several *hot* waitresses that worked here at the new place, but it wasn't the right time. "So, is Jane still moving?" Andy nodded, "How long?"

"Two weeks."

"Hmm." Mick was going to say *not long*, but that was blatantly and painfully obvious. He struggled to find anything to say that might cheer Andy up. Sometimes there just were no words available to do that. It was obvious to him that Andy hadn't visited him for the chat, more likely he called just to be around someone familiar. Mick flitted back and forth between the work he needed to do and chatting to Andy at the back door. An hour flew by, then they arranged to meet for a pint in the next few days. Then Andy set off to pick Fran up from the party.

◆ ◆ ◆

This time he parked up a little out of view of the living room window, and he focused his mind on something very specific; putting all the *other* stuff to the side for the moment. By the time he rang the doorbell, he'd managed to empty his mind of all the negative stuff bouncing around in there. Natalia's mum answered the door with a smile.

"Fran's dad." Andy said.

"Yes, hi. Thank you for bringing her, she's told us a lot about you today."

"Oh, really? Most of it good I hope."

"Oh certainly."

Behind the pleasant lady were just three kids, one being Fran, who greeted him. "My dad's here."

"Do you want to come in?" Natalia's mum asked; though he'd already taken two steps inside.

Natalia was sat on a chair on one side of the room; she had the oxygen mask on, “Natty needs a bit of help with her breathing sometimes, it’s been a bit much for her today...some of the other children her age find it a little *off-putting.*” she said quietly to Andy, “Your Fran doesn’t seem to notice.”

The party was over a little earlier than planned. The other children present started gathering their coats and putting their shoes on, ready for home. Andy said nothing, but took a few steps forward and held his hand out towards the birthday girl.

“Nice to meet you Natalia.” he said. She didn’t respond much, but smiled a little.

“She’s very tired at the minute.” her mum said, "She will perk up a bit later on." Andy smiled. He bent down slightly and touched Natalia on the hand. Her mum thought it a nice gesture, if a tiny bit odd. Natalia took a deeper breath, all of a sudden. Andy noticed a twinkle in her eye for a split second. He stood upright.

“Well, thanks for inviting Fran. I’m sure she’ll tell me all about it on the way home.” Andy said.

“She’s been a delight. She’s joined in all the games and the songs.”

Fran chirped up. “Look dad, I’ve won this at pass the parcel.” She showed Andy a miniature doll’s house gift.

“She enjoyed playing that one the most.” Natalia’s mum commented.

Fran picked up her piece of birthday cake; there seemed to be a lot left over, probably due to the small number of guests that had turned up. Andy accepted a piece for himself and then they said their goodbyes.

"Did you have a good time?" he asked on the way back to the car.

"Yes. I feel a bit sad for Nat. Only one other girl came from school."

"Oh...how many all together?"

Fran counted them. "Five. One was her sister and one the girl from next door."

"Well five is better than four."

"I suppose. Are we stopping at your house tonight?"

"Your mum said it was....no, I was just taking you to the party." He *had* asked Jane.

"Oh. ok."

Andy knew that Jane could have let the kids stay over if she felt so inclined, especially with them moving so soon. It was more punishment. She had the knife in him and was showing no signs of pulling it out; more likely she would give it another twist.

As he lifted Fran out of the car seat, he had a fleeting notion: he hoped this warm hearted little girl would not be influenced and changed by current and future events. Andy viewed her dark hearted mother as something toxic. *Show me the child at seven and I will show you the adult.* He couldn't remember exactly who had said that or how true a statement it was. Fran was still a way off age seven. Jack was seven. Without the *proper* family unit, they stood less chance of growing up unscathed. He would just have to do whatever he could at his end; consoling himself with the idea that no-one got the perfect upbringing.

# 22

Ten days till the move. Sue's friendly face popped around the kitchen door. She asked how Andy was and then told him about a new arrival coming soon.

"I'll bring the paperwork in later." she said. She did notice Andy's less than buoyant countenance, "Eric tells me your children are moving away."

"Yes." Andy stopped chopping for a moment.

"That can't be easy. How do you feel about that?"

"To be honest, I'm pretty gutted. But there's not a lot I can do about it."

Sue did look genuinely concerned. Andy's extra intuition was very useful for discerning whether emotions were authentic or not. "Well, you know." she said, "Dominic is a brilliant psychologist. One of the perks of working here is access to free counselling...should we need it. I'm not sure it's your thing, but he really helped me cope with the death of my dad."

"Oh." Andy instinctively knew that he would not be taking up that opportunity. Sue could see that on his face.

"Has he been in to see you often?"

"Er...no not really."

"I'm sure he's just been too busy."

"I've seen him coming and going." Andy did wonder why everyone, with the exception of Eric, thought the sun shined out of this guy's arse. He gave off a mixed vibe; his aura was all jumbled up. He trusted Sue, but didn't feel that he knew her well enough yet to say anything further.

Sure enough, Sue appeared later, holding a sealed envelope, which was a little bit different than normal procedure. The word *confidential* in red ink was on the envelope. "It's for a special patient." she said, quietly.

"Special?"

"I can't say any more than that."

"Oh, ok." Andy glimpsed at the name at the top of the sheet. *Was that the politician?* It would explain the confidential envelope and the *special* tag.

"It is strictly confidential." Sue said, "We don't, or rather *they* don't really want any press involvement."

"So it is the same one then."

"Between you and me...yes, but I didn't tell you that." she said, with a wry smile. Andy gave her a half-smile in return. The well known politician must've been desperate/open minded to need the Haven's alternative methods. Word of the miraculous healings was getting out there, even to rarefied heights.

Andy noted down his dietary requirements and then passed the document back to Sue. He hadn't had the chance to turn over the strip of paper that concealed his reason for being there. Sue bustled off again to continue her duties. She was the glue that held the place together....Dom *thought* he was.

◆ ◆ ◆

The next day, Andy was sifting through the contents of the larder and trying to decide what kind of soup to make, when Eric showed up at the kitchen back door. His singing alerted Andy to his presence, it was a bit off tune, but that did not deter Eric. It was always good to see him.

"Hey, what brings you here today?"

"Had an hour to kill. Wife's out shopping and I don't like standing around outside the changing room while she takes ages to try stuff on; looks like I'm loitering."

Andy laughed. "Let me get you a coffee." He went out to the machine; John was polishing the cafe floor and he waved to him. Eric was waiting for the coffee amidst a cloud of cigarette smoke, "Here you go." Andy said, as he looked at the burning cigarette. It was a new, quite hard and fast rule that there was to be no smoking on the premises. Eric noticed Andy's concern.

"Screw it. Rules and regulations. *Car park,* now *smoking ban.* No one else is breathing it in." Eric said. Andy shrugged; he knew that Eric's lungs had been *reset,* "Hey guess who I've just seen on the car park. Dead spit of him anyway." Andy knew who Eric was referring to, if it was the same person from the document he'd seen earlier. "Tony...whatever his second name is."

"Shhh." said Andy, "But between you and me, it *is* him. He's having treatment here."

"Really, it is? I thought that was why he had a bodyguard with him."

"He's gluten free."

"Hopefully he'll be gone by the next time I'm working." Eric said, as he stepped on the cigarette.

◆ ◆ ◆

Six days till the move. Andy was standing waiting for Fran in the fine drizzle rain. It's the last weekday he will be in this position: next week they would be gone. Fran came bounding out of the doors as soon as they opened.

"Dad, dad, guess what?!"

"What is it?" For a fleeting moment, he flirted with the idea that she might be telling him that the move was off. He looked up at the sky and noticed a rainbow that had been there for a while.

"Dad, do you know the girl from the party. She doesn't need the mask anymore." On cue, Natalia came out of the school door, unaided and smiling. She gave Fran a hug and then joined her mother. It'd been a few days and Andy had forgotten that he had healed her at the party.

"That's great news Fran."

"Yes, she's all better. She's coming to my house on Saturday." Then Fran shrugged, "Before we leave."

Andy smiled. He looked up at the rainbow; it was still there, but had faded slightly. He wondered whether or not he should mention to her that this would be the last time he would collect her from school. Instead, he said.

"So, what would you like for tea?" She pondered on this as Jack came out to join them.

"What do you want for tea?" she asked her brother. Jack was aware that this would be the last time dad would collect them.

"I don't mind." he replied.

Andy asked them to decide on the way back. They could choose anything that they wanted.

They ended up going to the chip shop and eating out of the paper on the dining room table. With every chip eaten, Andy tried to console himself with the notion that it wasn't the last time he would see them, it would just be more infrequent. *A fresh start* is how Jane had put it. He wondered how she would feel if the shoe was on the other foot.

Andy felt very low, like something good was coming to an end, which it was. He still couldn't help but smile at Fran's enthusiasm as she did the little everyday things. She was a bit too young to feel what Jack was feeling, though he was trying his best not to show it, Andy could read what he was feeling. *It could be worse.* Andy found himself repeating that line a lot lately. He tried to shift his focus to his *job* of healing people, which he had been handed on a golden platter. *Where had that one in a million chance been all the times he had done the lottery.* His own personal priorities seemed to have less significance than they had *pre-gift*, and the main thing was that the kids were fit and healthy. They might even appreciate the move...in time, whether he did or not. He told himself all  of this, without really believing it as much as he would have liked. One thing about having the gift was that, not only could he read other people more accurately, he could also read himself much better and he always flagged up any of the little lies we all tell ourselves....white or black. Now, he could look back on some of his own actions over the years and see his *real* motivation for them...which wasn't always good to know. *He was only human*, he consoled himself and he tried not to ruminate on these less than perfect deeds.

Later, after feeling like he'd just taken part in

an extremely watered down version of the *last supper,* Andy dropped the kids back off with Jane. She didn't bother coming out of the house. Andy drove away as they went through the front door; this time it felt too painful to wait and watch them wave from the window.

# 23

Four days till the move. The former politician was still at the Haven receiving treatment, though not staying overnight. Andy was not a keen follower of politics or even a follower at all. He knew the different parties, who all seemed equally as bad as each other. He only ever voted if it wasn't raining and he felt in the mood. All of them seemed as false as Dom. He did know about this particular guy though, more or less everyone in the UK did, unless they had been living in a cave. *Weapons of mass destruction.....did he know they had none all along?*

At 10:00 am, Andy sat at one end of the café with John. He didn't often get a chance for a break, but he had been working at double speed, fuelled by nervous energy, so he was two steps ahead in his preparation. John was in his usual laid back state of mind. The jury was still out on whether Andy felt resentful or grateful or somewhere in between, regarding inheriting the gift from him.

"You heard about the new guest?" Andy asked him.

"Yes. Supposed to be a secret isn't it."

"What do you think of him?"

"I don't know, I no longer see auras, but I thought he was a prat before."

"I haven't seen him in person yet. I'm getting more used to reading these auras though; they seem to have different shades of colour."

"Yeah. The main thing I found is to just let it appear to you; the *essence* of a person is always there to see. Even without the gift, people don't trust their gut as much as they should do. It's a forgotten art. *Civilisation* has done that." John smiled as he took a sip of organic tea.

"It is...but just think how all our lives would be different if everyone listened to their gut *all* the time."

"Maybe they shouldn't then."

"Well, perhaps if we knew when *not* to listen, we would be still listening to our gut."

John laughed. "It's not easy is it, this whole *life* deal."

"Maybe it is for some people."

"Not really...just different people different problems. Even the rich and famous."

"I'll take the problem of having to decide which Ferrari to buy." Andy joked.

"You have the gift now....every day that goes by, you know a little more about what it's all about." At the other end of the café, the former politician, who was the low-key talk of the Haven, was showed to a table, "Look who's there." John said.

"Look who's with him." Andy noticed Dom buzzing around the new arrival. He rarely appeared with the patients. Dom looked over and noticed John sat with Andy, he stopped, staring for a few seconds in the same manner a lion might at an antelope.

"Better get back to work; big brother is watching us." John said.

"I don't think us taking time out is his reason for taking such notice." Andy replied, "He still hasn't been in to say hello."

"He is an acquired taste. An expensive wine that that's gone off. Do you pick up on his aura?"

"Not really...he's difficult to read. It's almost like he doesn't exist."

"Some people are like that...the false ones. Anyway, he's gone now and I'd better get back to work. Don't think I'm being nosey, but have you thought about healing thepolitician?"

"What do you think...should I?"

"Hey, it's up to you. Look, I'll catch you later. I'm glad you seem to be coming to terms with what I did and what you have." John got up and left the table.

"Slowly but surely. Bye for now John." Andy replied.

He took a look across the café and realised that it was now just him and the new arrival: the café wasn't officially open until 12:00. Andy made a choice and got up out of his chair. He walked over to where the v.i.p. was reading the newspaper, in-between treatments. "Hello." he said.

The retired politician looked up and replied. "Hello, you must be the chef." It was pretty obvious from Andy's uniform.

"Yes, nice to meet you." *Was it really?* Andy outstretched his hand; it was grasped in a well practiced, firm but *empty* grip. Andy felt a tingle of electricity, and then he saw....for just a fleeting moment....many faces of anguish, pain and tears; devastated and desolate buildings; crying children, explosions and wailing women. He retracted his hand.

"Are you alright?" The v.i.p. asked him. He had felt nothing out of the ordinary, but he'd noticed Andy's expression had altered.

"Yes."

"Something concerning you?"

"No, I'm fine. I'd better get back and ready for lunch."

"What's hot and spicy? I know I shouldn't, but I'm in the mood."

Andy had another flash image of fire and burning buildings...what seemed like a whole city on fire. "The organic chilli is pretty hot. I could add a bit of spice to it if you want." Then he lied spontaneously, "Nice to have met you. Hope you enjoy lunch." He turned and headed back to the kitchen. The v.i.p. smiled and continued reading his newspaper.

# 24

Three days before the move. Andy woke at the sound of an inconsiderate cuckoo that wasn't aware of or didn't care about the time. He got up, looked out of the bedroom window and surveyed the dark grey sky. Today was going to be straight forward. No patients: the former politician's symptoms were gone; they disappeared soon after the handshake. Andy never did find out what they were. *Over active conscience*? Eric was in at lunchtime to help and Carol was going to be in the office. He would go in and say hi to her and then play it by ear... not jump to any conclusions or foster any expectations.

He set off to work with a coffee placed in the car's cup holder; the fifteen minute journey seemed all the better with a coffee. The new windscreen wiper wasn't a perfect fit...he never could get them to fit perfectly, but it was doing its job well enough as the rain was starting to come down continuously. The roads were always fairly quiet at this time in the morning, which was one advantage of starting work early. Andy tended to drive conservatively, that way his Ford could get forty miles on a gallon of fuel, not bad for its age and with money being tight, these little things made a difference.

About half way into the journey, he hit an incline in the road, the spot where he normally had to drop down into third gear. As he did so, in between the sweeping motion of the rear view wipers, he saw a black car right up close behind him, filling the rear view mirror. The black car flashed it's lights as though to hurry him up or prompt him to get out of the way. Andy wasn't able to go much faster…they would have to wait. The black car's lights flashed again, twice, then there was a quick beep of the horn, followed by a long beep. *Impatient prat.* Then, through the rear window, he saw that the car was a BMW and in the driver's seat was Rick, who had recognized Andy's Ford and was smiling a really unpleasant, smarmy looking grin. Andy wasn't going to speed up, especially not for this bastard. Then, with another flash of it's lights, the BMW roared past with another *beep* and a glance to his left from Rick, flashing that creepy, smug smile to Andy. When he had shot past, Andy saw Rick's eyes in the BMW's rear view mirror, mocking him. Then, suddenly, the BMW twitched on the road, it was travelling too fast and a rain filled pot hole snagged the front right wheel. Perhaps if Rick and been looking ahead, instead of in the rear view at Andy, he might have seen it. The black BMW span around as though in slow motion, hit a dry stone wall and then flipped twice, as though it was defying gravity, before coming to rest back on its roof, completely stationary, with steam coming out of it and its side indicators blinking. Andy stopped his Ford just behind it. There were no other cars on the road. From the rear the BMW looked upended, but relatively undamaged. Andy got out, the rain steadily pouring off his hair and face as he walked over to the black car. As he got closer, he could see parts of it all bent out of shape; closer still and he could see the twisted and exposed bare silver metal from the crash. Inside, Rick was motionless, still in the driver seat. To Andy's massive relief, no one else was in the car with him. The airbag had deployed but had then been punctured by broken metal. The windscreen was smashed, as were the front windows. Rick had blood on his face and in his hair, but his eyes flickered and were open. He was breathing very lightly. Andy looked at this injured, broken looking man for several seconds. Rick turned his eyes slightly to look at him, the expression on his face in stark contrast to the mocking one from just a few moments ago. Andy reached through the broken window...he could touch Rick from here. He extended his hand so far and then abruptly stopped, just inches away. It seemed like an eternity passed, but it was actually only several seconds. Behind him, another driver had seen the accident and also stopped. Putting his hazard lights on, the other driver got out and jogged over to the BMW.

"Have you called the services yet?" the other driver asked Andy. Andy withdrew his hand from the window.

"No, it's only just happened."

"I'll do it. Is he still alive?"

"Yes, I think so."

The other driver made the call and they both waited in the rain. The other driver asked what had happened; Andy told him that the BMW span out of control. He repeated the story to the services when they arrived on the scene and the Police asked him to make a statement. The ambulance arrived and the fire brigade had to cut off the door of the BMW so that they could get Rick out. Sparks flew everywhere, like a firework display. Rick was loaded into the ambulance and the black BMW status symbol got towed away.

Andy could have healed Rick but he hadn't done. He didn't feel bad about that, he hadn't caused the crash, but *perhaps* he had delayed the big move for a while and maybe, just maybe, Jane would change her mind.

Andy called Eric to tell him what had happened and to expect him a little later, Eric told him it was no problem and went in early to set up the kitchen.

Andy arrived in sombre mood; he had a feeling he'd never had before, he was trying to assimilate it and recognize what the feeling was. It was like his body wasn't working in unison with his head. As he was working, he spilt a couple of things, knocked something else over, dropped a plate and was generally clumsy. It took till lunchtime till he felt almost back to normal... whatever normal had become.

"You're in shock." Eric said, when he knocked a bowl of lentil soup over, "Why don't you go home and let me do today. It's fine." Andy had no clue to how Rick was doing and it was all that he could think about.

"I'll do service with you till two and then see... thanks pal." Andy said. He worked at less than his normal snappy speed and Eric picked up the slack. He knew that Rick had sped past him to prove a point, a childish prank to prove he was superior. He wondered what Rick was thinking now. Andy did hate this man, the one who had turned his wife's head and was the root cause of his children moving to another part of the country. But Jane shared the blame. If it wasn't Rick, it would have been somebody else.

There was no one at the Haven that needed healing and Andy went the whole day without using his power. He went home at 3:00pm and fell asleep for a few hours, waking at 6:00pm with the idea to go out and wander around till he eventually found someone that needed him before the end of the day. But he didn't. He had a knot in his stomach and a strange feeling he didn't much care for.

◆ ◆ ◆

The next day, Saturday, was his day off work and he was due to pick the kids up around noon. As they were planning to leave very soon, Jane had actually agreed to let Andy see the kids on a day that he didn't normally, it was just about the only concession that she had made. Andy had planned to take them to the park and feed the ducks, one of their favourite things to do.

When he got to the house, the black BMW was gone, as expected, it was probably a write-off. He waited for Jane to come out of the house, *would she tell him about the accident? Did she know he was at the scene?* If she did, he hoped she didn't think the crash was his fault. He would, at the very least, have a few more weeks with the kids whilst Rick recovered. Jane came out of the house slowly; the kids ran past her and got into Andy's car.

"There's been an accident." she said, "Rick is dead."

"Dead?"

"His car crashed; he died from his injuries before he got to the hospital." Jane said. Andy was not expecting that; Rick had looked banged up a bit, but not critical. In the next five seconds he had five minutes worth of feelings, one of which was satisfaction…he couldn't escape that. He had no idea how to respond, so he didn't, "Bring them back before three tomorrow would you." Jane said, before heading back inside.

All Andy could say was. "Ok."

In the car, the kids looked a little bemused; they hadn't had the experience of losing someone before, even though they had known Rick only a few months. Jack, in particular, looked deep in thought.

"Are you ok Jack?" Andy asked. Jack nodded.

"Does this mean we don't have to go away?" Jack asked.

"We will talk about it a bit later pal. Is that ok?" Jack nodded again.

They stopped off at the river bank got out and took in some fresh air. Andy had brought some bread with him and the ducks came waddling over to be fed. This was one consistent activity that they had kept up for the last couple of years, a *go to* if they had no other plans. And it was free, which helped as Andy did not have a lot of money. Somehow this simple activity felt reassuring, today especially.

"Dad, can we get some ducks at your house?" Fran asked, out of the blue.

"I don't think they would be comfortable.

They need water." Andy replied.

"Well I have a paddling pool at home; I could bring it to your house." Fran added.

"One could fit in the bath." suggested Jack.

"We could take one with us. What about that one?" Fran pointed at one particular duck.

"I'm not sure it would be fair on the duck Fran. If I get a bigger house, we can think about it." Andy said.

Naturally, the ducks had no idea of their therapeutic influence. It was all serenely quiet for a while, apart from the sound of the odd bird chirping, the ducks quacking and the splashing of water.

◆ ◆ ◆

The rest of the night was spent in front of the tv and games console. Andy ordered a pizza delivery and also invited Mick around. It felt good to see him when he answered the door, complete with four beers in hand. They spoke in the hallway whilst the kids were playing on a game.

"What's the big news then?" Mick asked.

"You are not going to believe it." Andy wasn't going to tell him the news of the healing power, not yet at least,"That guy is dead."

"Who's dead? What guy?"

"Rick…Jane's boyfriend. He has died in a car crash."

"Christ."

"I saw it happen, he had just gone flying past me, then he rolled it."

"Good."

"Bit harsh man."

"Nah, he was a dick from what you were saying. *Dick* by name, *dick* by nature." Andy couldn't or didn't feel like arguing the point. "This means they won't be leaving now, right?" Mick said.

"Maybe not."

"So, good, he got what he deserved, splitting up a family like that." Andy felt only a little regret about not saving Rick, *next to none.* "Don't tell me you feel sorry for him?" Mick asked.

"No, that's just it. I don't. Not a bit."

"That's the way you need to look at it. Shame about the accident, was anyone else hurt?"

"No."

"Then fine, don't give people like him a second thought." Mick handed him a can of beer and they both took a swig. In a way it felt like they were toasting Rick's death, "One less asshole in the world." Andy possibly should have, but did not find that comment from Mick distasteful.

They spent an hour or so talking about various subjects, Mick's latest job and girlfriend opportunities featuring quite heavily. It felt good to Andy to have some normality after all the recent upheavals and mind blowing, unreal seeming events. Mick had a *grounding* quality. Andy *almost* told him about the other giant sized news: the healing power, but put that on the back burner, for now.

◆ ◆ ◆

The next day the kids seemed a bit chirpier and almost back to normal: most kids are more resilient than adults. The drive to drop them back off felt different this time; there was no Rick lurking around in the background and Andy knew that, in terms of not seeing the kids, he'd been given a reprieve. A suspended sentance. Jane came out of the house when he pulled up, lacking the recent cockiness, but still cold and distant. She looked pale.

"How were they?" she asked.

"Fine." Andy said. He wondered for a second if Jane thought the kids had grown more attached to Rick than they actually had, it was only a matter of months they had been together; or at least that's what she had said. He resisted the temptation to say that *Jack couldn't stand the prick*; instead he arranged the next stop over and that was all. He looked at Jane one last time before he set off back. There was no chance of them ever getting back together, especially after him seeing the almost reptilian side to her that had, spookily, probably always been there in the eight years that they had spent together. He felt no pity for her either...that avenue had a roadblock in front of it. This woman had caused and was about to cause him even more immeasurable pain without even giving it a second's thought. The kids waved to him as he drove off.

He called in at the supermarket on the way home, drifting around the aisles, deep in thought, picking up various bits and pieces, just wanting to be around people. He bought another half bottle of whiskey before he left: something to try and take the edge of this very odd and unpleasant feeling he'd had for the last day or so. He made a deal with himself that he wouldn't buy any more for a while after this: becoming an alcoholic was probably not going to aid him in any way.

# 25

Andy took a different route to work the next day, avoiding the stretch of road where the accident had taken place. When he arrived, he picked up a note from Eric telling him that he was going to stay on part-time for the foreseeable future, as he was enjoying it now. Many people would have simply texted the message, but Eric was *old school.* This was great news to Andy and lifted his mood a little. The note also mentioned a new patient *Alison Green,* her notes said that she had a tumour that was inoperable; no other treatment was available and the Haven was, sadly, her last option. She was still mobile and able to come down to the café at lunchtimes and in-between treatments. Andy wanted to help her as soon as he could, hoping that deed would cancel out the sour taste he still had in his mouth about Rick. He wanted to bury that decision under an avalanche of good deeds.

He sipped a coffee and wondered why he had a hangover from the whiskey. *Never get ill* was the mantra, *did this count as being ill?*

Before long, Alison's order for lunch came through and he began preparing it for when she showed up in the café. At noon exactly, she arrived with some help from the Haven's staff. She looked weak but in surprisingly good spirits. She sat at a window table and took in the view of the Haven's cultured grounds. Before long, her empty plate came back through to the kitchen. *Empty plate* was always a good sign. Andy chose his moment and took off the blue latex food-prep glove from his right hand; he went straight over to her table before she moved back upstairs.

"Hi, I am Andy, the chef here. How was your lunch?" he asked.

"Very nice. I managed to eat most of it." she said, in a clear but slightly strained voice.

"Good, if there is anything special that you fancy that isn't on the menu just let the staff know and I'll see what I can do." Alison smiled. Andy saw an opportunity to make skin contact with her and he placed his hand on hers just for a second, whilst having the intention to heal. *That should do it,* he thought. *She seemed like a nice lady.* He went back to the kitchen feeling a little better, but still carrying that odd feeling that he couldn't quite identify.

◆ ◆ ◆

Service was busy today. The news item had started to increase numbers in the organic cafe. At one point all the tables were full and Andy had to move into top gear to keep up, something he hadn't needed to do for a while. *Still got it,* he thought as the last of the meals went out of the kitchen. Just before he finished his shift, whilst he was sweeping the kitchen floor, he looked out of the kitchen window. In the Haven's grounds a staff member was pushing a wheelchair around. As there was only one patient at the moment, it had to be Alison. *Not an immediate cure.* He shrugged it off and finished sweeping and mopping. He flicked the lights out, leaving just the neon glow of the insectocuter, and took the alternate route home again.

◆ ◆ ◆

The next day he fully expected to see that Alison was either gone or walking around looking healthy. She turned up at noon in the café, still in a wheelchair and looking, if anything, slightly worse than the previous day. *It didn't seem to have worked.* He immediately resolved to go out again and repeat the process at the earliest opportunity. At midday, he got a second chance, and this time he left his hand on hers for slightly longer, as they were chatting, hopefully without it looking odd. He concentrated fully on helping her. *Surely this time.* There was no immediate change; in fact, she spoke very wearily in jerky sentences. Outside of the window, John was in the grounds, clearing away some leaves and doing general maintenance; he had seen Andy's puzzled look and had taken a mental note of it. He caught up with him at the kitchen's back door during a lull in service.

"Everything ok Andy?" John asked.

"I'm not sure. It didn't work on that lady, Alison. I tried a second time today, but there's no change in her yet. It usually works straight away, more or less. Was it that way with you?"

"Yes, more or less. What does she have?"

"A tumour." Andy said.

John looked deep in thought as he remembered his own similar circumstance when the cure *was* successful.

"You had the intention to heal?" Andy nodded, "Has anything happened?"

"What do you mean?" replied Andy.

"Anything about the gift, or just anything out of the ordinary?"

"There is something." Andy said, at length.

"Go on."

"I had the chance, the oppurtunity, to heal someone."

"But you didn't?"

"No. No I didn't and...now they are dead."

"What was the reason you didn't heal them?"

Andy sighed. “It was my wife’s boyfriend. He was in a crash and I was there.”

“The reason you didn’t heal him, was the fact that he was your ex-wife’s partner?”

“To be honest, I hated the guy. It was his fault that she was moving away with my kids, but I honestly didn’t expect him to die from the injuries he had.”

“I see.” John, again, looked deep in thought.

“Did you ever choose *not* to heal anyone?” Andy asked. John did not reply, but his lack of a reply suggested that his answer would have been *no*, “What is it?” Andy noticed the thoughtful look on John’s face, “Have I lost the power to heal because of this?” John concentrated carefully, and then said.

“I was warned when I got it, not to use it selfishly. Whatever else is a bit blurry, it’s decades ago.”

“Could you contact whoever passed it on to you? Maybe they would know something else?”

“Peter? I could try...assuming he is still alive. We have not spoken in about a year, which is not great on my part. Leave it with me.”

Andy left work thinking this might actually be a blessing...losing the ability to heal, if that’s what had happened. He could go back to being just *plain old Andy.* The odd feeling still remained though, almost like something under his skin troubled him.

Later that night, he sat with the tv on low with a Jack Daniels in hand, mulling over events on repeat. He wondered if there was something he had missed; another piece to the jigsaw somewhere. As he was sitting there he received a message from Carol, asking him how he was. It was now a few days since their encounter and many more events had happened since that had already faded the memory of it. He complimented her cooking and they agreed to do it again sometime, perhaps he would cook, though he would have to go on a major cleaning spree in his flat first...and possibly buy some new plates and cutlery. He didn't tell her that bit. He texted that he would speak to her next time she was in the office.

Then his phone rang...it was John. He had previously explained to Andy that he hadn't spoken or contacted Peter at all in the last year, probably because Peter's Alzheimer's distressed him.

"I spoke to Peter." John said, "Luckily he hadn't changed his number and is alive and well, apart from the Alzheimer's. He was in a good moment, the best I have heard him in a long time. There *is* something you need to know."

"What is it?"

"He was a bit sketchy at first, and then he seemed to remember quite clearly; he said that *if the gift is used selfishly it can stop. Not only that, it can be reversed*. He said it had never happened with him, but he had heard of it through another with the gift. He said, in his words, the *touch of life* could become the *touch of death*. Mind you, he is eighty eight years old and may be confused."

"Touch of death...you're kidding? What do you mean by that?"

"You don't cure someone when you touch them, you...well, the opposite happens."

Andy had a flashback to how Alison looked the day after his cure attempt; she had seemed worse. He said nothing for a few seconds, then. "What do I do?"

"Have you made skin contact with anyone else?" John asked.

"I don't know. I wear the blue gloves at work." Then Andy remembered he had the kids over to stay recently and it dawned on him like a ton of bricks, "My kids stayed over one time... since the crash."

"Did they seem ok when you took them back the next day?" John asked.

"They seemed fine, as far as I could tell."

"Hopefully, all will be well. Just keep the food preperation gloves on till we know more. I'll try and do some  more research. Peter also told me that he, I, and now you, were not the only one."

"There are other people with this gift?"

"There are. Don't touch anyone for now." John said and then he ended the call.

# 26

John had been looking forward to retirement; he certainly wasn't dreading it like some people did: quite often, they were the ones who didn't like their own company. Only a few weeks to go and the day would finally arrive and he had a list of things that he wanted to do, more or less in order. That was his type of character: everything in order if at all possible. The boring stuff, like painting walls and brickwork was on the list of stuff to do, but the number one, in terms of the things that he was looking forward to, was to buy a boat of some kind and take it to different places around the coast. Catch some fish, though the fish were not the priority. How big a boat he wanted or could afford, he hadn't yet decided. He sometimes wondered that if he had charged a fee for all the healings he had done over the years, like Dom had with his fanciful faith-healing sessions, then it might possibly be a twenty five foot yacht.

That was not how the deal went; Peter had told him right at the beginning that healing for personal gain would go against the unwritten rules of the gift. Exactly who or what had come up with these rules or guidelines was unknown. Some kind of *higher* power, no doubt. He was advised, way back then, not to try and work it out, just accept it as it was and go with the flow.

He had been careful with his money during his working life, he lived fairly frugally and he never got involved with anyone else after he split with his second wife, at least no one that he felt he wanted to make a commitment to. He never felt lonely; he was at peace with himself and was quite happy with his music and hobbies.

He saw his children from his first marriage regularly: at the very least every Christmas and Easter. His first wife had died during childbirth, there had been complications. He had never told his daughter that he'd made the choice, whether to save her or her mother. Of course he would *never* say that. *Why burden her as well*. It haunted him every day though, the choice, but once he had decided, he knew that he would have to live with that decision for the rest of his life. At that precise moment in time, he hated the *once per day* rule, but at least he was able to save one of them.

John knew that he had acted purely on instinct when passing on the gift to Andy. The *never get Ill* perk of having the gift was a big thing to give up, but he had known it was time to pass it on, just as Peter had known it was time to pass it on to him. What he had not expected, however, were the complications that had arisen so soon after doing so, and this troubled him greatly. He felt responsible. Peter had been a priest, he had thought the gift was something special passed straight down from God. Peter had passed it to John, not because of his religious name, but because he had seen the golden aura around him, brighter than he had in any other person in over three decades.

John was piecing together what he could remember; stuff that he thought he would never need to recall again. His time with the gift had gone textbook smooth and that made these recent events even more unexpected. According to the recent conversation with Peter, there were several people across the globe with this same gift, one on each continent or so he remembered. One of whom surely would have more information on this reversal of fortune. They needed advice on what they should do; this was not a situation where the answer was in a textbook or on the internet. This was a secret society in the extreme and Peter, God bless him, was suffering with Alzheimer's and only made coherent sense occasionally. If he had kept the never get ill bonus from the gift, that might not have become the case. John wondered briefly what fate may await *him*, now that he hadn't got the never get ill perk. *All par for the course though,* he concluded. That was for the future to decide.

Using the power of *Google* and on-line forums, he searched for any information available on others with the gift. Searches brought up so many links, that it was going to take a long while to sort the wheat from the chaff, if indeed there was any wheat at the end of it. In all the time that he'd had it, it had never occurred to him to search for others that might also possess the same gift. He had just taken every day as it came and assumed it was just him.

The vast majority of the claims on the internet *had* to be fake and he supposed that the more outrageous and glossy the reports, the more likely they were to be so. It had to be the needle in the haystack, the one person not doing it for personal gain or fortune. After many hours searching, he narrowed it down to half a dozen more likely candidates; completely ignoring *how much can you make as a healer*? Or *how to become a faith healer*. But even these candidates seemed unlikely. The vast majority claiming to have a healing gift were obviously fakes, performing in front of crowds of thousands, just like the evangelical con-men sometimes seen on tv in the states.

There was no mention anywhere, of an ability that could jump from person to person. The most infamous faith healer from South America was securely in jail, so he was crossed off the list. It had to be someone undercover as he himself had been, which meant, by default, they were going to be hard to find. Then, unexpectedly, John received a call from Peter who in another one of his better moments had remembered something else.

"Those other healers you were asking about. There's one in India, if he's still alive. He had the gift since he was twenty years old; now he must be in his eighties. From what I remember... never looked like passing it on. Lived in the north east, name *Ramesh*, known locally by some as *the righteous one*. He never left his home village. I met him once." Peter said. He didn't explain where or when or why the meeting happened. He didn't remember.

John thanked Peter for his help and bid him goodnight. John wondered if he would ever speak to Peter in that lucid state again; he hoped so, but perhaps that information was to be Peter's parting gift. A further search for both *Ramesh* and *the righteous one* delivered few results, but there was something. In an on-line forum, dated last year, someone in that same region of India had claimed to have been healed of some condition or other and used the phrase *the righteous one*, describing the healer briefly as an old man. If this man in India did indeed still have the power, then he could well live to a ripe old age as he would never get ill. This character was obviously not flaunting or publicising his ability because there was *nothing* else on him.....exactly the way it should have been. Interestingly, this forum was still active and the author of the comment was available to contact. John sent him a message. Of course, it was possible that Peter had imagined the whole thing, but John instinctively knew that he hadn't.

◆ ◆ ◆

Andy had taken John's advice and was now wearing the blue gloves constantly. He was about to call Jane to cancel having the kids over at the weekend, till he could be sure what was going on. He was going to tell her that he did't feel well, which was kind of true, so not really a lie. He called her number, which still gave him a weird feeling every time he did it.

"Hi, Jane it's me. Look I'm sorry it's short notice, but it might be better if we cancel the kids this weekend as I'm not feeling great."

"What's wrong with you?" Jane asked.

"Just feeling like crap."

"Its fine, I was going to call you anyway...Fran is not feeling well. We have literally just got back from the doctors."

"What is it?"

"They don't know. They have done some tests and we get the results back tomorrow. Might be glandular they say. She's really washed out."

Andy said nothing for a few seconds. “When did this start? Is she getting any worse?” he asked, trying to sound calm.

“She doesn’t seem to be getting any better, since she came back from yours. I thought you may have had the same thing, a bug or something.”

“I haven’t been to the doctor, you know I don’t like going. Keep me posted would you please, I would like to know what the tests say?”

“I’ll ring you tomorrow.” Jane said.

“Wait,…is Jack ok?”

“Yes he’s fine.”

“Bye.”

Andy had a flashback to when the kids were staying over recently. He did give Fran a hug: Jack didn’t like hugs much so generally he got a pat on the head. Andy hoped this illness of Fran’s was a coincidence and nothing to do with the gift reversal, if indeed that's what was happening. He prayed that the tests came back with a rational explanation.

John called Andy about an hour later with the update from his research. He told him about the information from Peter and the link to the healer in India, the rest of the other options seemingly being charlatans.

“India.” repeated Andy, “Hardly just around the corner. Does Peter know anything else about what might have happened?”

"No, he doesn't, though he did seem crystal clear on the memory of Ramesh. If anyone knows the way to proceed, it would be him, as he has kept the gift more or less all his life, from age twenty." The memory of Ramesh had appeared like a brief oasis of clarity in the sometimes empty desert of Peter's often confused state, "This reversal of your power was caused partly by fate and perhaps fate has helped Peter remember some detail about this man in India. As things stand, it's the only lead we have to go on. I did get a response from one of those on-line forums, from someone claiming to have been healed by this person...Ramesh. He confirmed that he existed and that he lives in a place called *Lucknow* in the north east of the country. He has even agreed to meet up, should we need him to."

It did seem a bit sketchy to Andy, but it was all they had to go on. His own digging had returned nothing but what seemed to be con artists or magicians.

"Ok. Will speak more at work tomorrow and John...thanks." Andy ended the call. He spent an hour checking out what John had just told him on his own laptop and concluded that it seemed like the only decent thread they had to follow. If anyone knew what was going on and also how to *solve* the problem, it would be this *Ramesh* in the aptly named *Lucknow* district of India...if he actually existed.

# 27

The next morning Andy received a call from Jane telling him that the test results for Fran were back from the surgery and that they didn't know what was wrong with her. They had suggested bringing her in once again, but this time to the hospital.

"Is she any worse?" Andy asked.

"She is very weak." Jane replied.

"Keep me up to date with any changes please; do you want me to come with you?"

"No it's not necessary. I will ring you with any updates." Jane did not want to spend any time with Andy. After Rick's death, she felt exposed and vulnerable. Andy would not use the situation to attack her, butstill, she wanted to keep her distance. She felt like someone who had taken the first pistol shot in a duel, and then missed. He came off the call feeling helpless. Because of the less than acrimonious split, he felt like he couldn't communicate with Jane properly, on an even keel. He wouldn't have wanted to in a *normal* situation, but this was different.

He wanted to speak with John again and was grateful when John arrived at work. When he got a free moment, he sought him out in the corridor.

"She's not getting any better." Andy told him.

John looked very concerned. "It's not good news. Alison has passed away, during the night." he said.

"Good God."

"She had deteriorated quite severely in the last two days."

"Oh my God, I've done this."

"We don't know that." John said.

"I have. I know I have."

"You say your daughter has gotten worse?"

"Yes, they are takening her into hospital. They can't identify what's wrong with her."

"We don't know for sure that the gift has been reversed."

"I do, somehow. I've had this odd uncomfortable feeling, like something crawling under my skin. I should never have let my own personal feelings interfere with this healing, but I should be allowed a second chance, shouldn't I? I didn't even ask for or want any of this. Now Alison is dead and Fran is suffering for my own selfishness. But, I honestly didn't expect him to die." Andy said forlornly, "What the hell can I do now?"

"The path is fairly clear. It looks like we have

only one option available. Of course, a way to be completely certain would be to touch someone else and see what happened to them."

"I can't take that chance and time is running out for Fran. I have to do something quick. Like right away."

"She is young and resilient, and we still don't know if she is affected or not. It might be just a coincidence." John said.

"I need to know as soon as possible. I have to go to India and find that Ramesh."

"It's a long shot."

"It is, but it's the only shot we have. I need to do it. I don't see another way. Somehow I know he exists, though what do I know."

"We know the district he is in. It is a shame we can't contact this Ramesh person directly, but there is that one person from the forum who lives there, he said he would take us to him if needed."

"Will you contact him please?"

"Sure. What about the flights, it's not going to be cheap?" John asked.

"I have the payout from my last job; that should cover it."

"I'll give you what you need."

"I can't take your money...it's *my* fault."

"I passed it on to you without your knowledge. Don't worry, I'll just get a smaller boat."

◆ ◆ ◆

Later in the kitchen, Andy asked Eric how he would feel about covering for him for a couple of days; Eric said it was fine; though Andy would have still gone anyway, he wanted to ask out of courtesy. Later, John came back with the good news that the guy in India from the forum who had been healed, would indeed meet up if needed, especially when motivated by the added incentive of a cash bonus promised for his trouble. They both knew that it wasn't anything concrete but it was all they had. If anyone knew how to resolve the problem it would be this *righteous one*, the one who had kept the same gift for sixty plus years. It was just a pity that they couldn't just call him to find out.

There was a direct flight from Manchester to Lucknow India, leaving tomorrow. Seats were available. At short notice it was £541. Andy booked it and dug out his passport which, fortunately, had seven months left until it expired. He hadn't expected to go anywhere abroad in the near future, and he breathed a massive sigh of relief when he saw that it was still valid. Jane called him later that day.

"They are keeping her in; they still don't know the cause of her illness and want to monitor her overnight. Can you get here? They are talking about placing her in an induced coma." Andy's heart sank even lower.

"I can't."

"What do mean you can't? This is important Andy."

"Look, I know, I really...*really* would if I could. I'll get there as soon as I can I promise, please trust me."

"Ok, whatever you are doing, just hurry it up."

Andy ended the call just as his doorbell rang; when he answered he saw John standing there and invited him in.

"They are keeping her in hospital." he told him.

John handed over a bundle of cash. "Here take this. I've already transferred a thousand to the account number you gave me. It clears straight away."

"I'll pay you back when I can."

"Forget that for now. Go and find this guy and see what he comes up with, if need be, bring him back with you."

Andy looked at this genuine guy and felt mixed emotions, he was doing all he could to help, but if he'd never laid eyes on him, none of this would be happening.

"Ok." Is all Andy could say. John passed him the number of the contact he has.

"I have texted you this as well. Ring him when you arrive in Lucknow. He will take you to

Ramesh."

"Ok."

"Let's get going, the flight is in two hours. I'll drive you to the airport." They left hurriedly and John waited briefly with Andy for the time to board. It was on schedule and not delayed, "Here." said John and he passed Andy two bottles of water, "It's very hot there, drink only bottled water." Andy nodded and before long he was stood in the queue and checking in.

"Any luggage sir?" They asked him at the checkpoint. Andy shook his head. The check-in staff member thought it a little odd, but she'd seen it all in twenty years, so someone flying to India with hardly any hand luggage, never mind cases, didn't cause much of a ripple. Within a short space of time, he was filing onto the plane, it was only ¾ full and he had an aisle seat. All the other passengers on the plane seemed to be casually going about their business. Andy had a slight *out of body* experience; he was looking down on himself from above. Then he was back looking through his own eyes. He tried to suppress a growing feeling of panic and kept his mind on the task at hand. Before long, the plane was in the air and the journey had begun.

# 28

In the basement of the Haven was Dom's favourite room, the *faith-healing room.* At first glance it might've reminded whoever saw it of a gothic scene from one of the old *Hammer Horror* films of the 1970's. In the centre was a heavy, ornately carved table. Candles in antique candelabra's were strategically placed around the dimly lit room. Carefully chosen symbols, artifacts and masks adorned the walls; all it really needed was a guest appearance by Count Dracula himself to complete the scene. Instead, they had Dom.

The simple, haunting, low key tones of whales communicating were humming gently as the patient was brought in and laid down on the centre table. This was to be no ritual virgin's sacrifice: it was a faith-healing session, with Dom in his favorite role, and taking centre stage.

The second healer due to take part had been delayed in traffic and so was unable to *perform*, so Dom had paid the office supplies delivery driver

£40 for him to take her place. He was instructed not to say a word about it, and told that if he played the part well and did as he was instructed, he would get more regular work. The driver looked like an old soul with a *lived-in* face that was exactly right for the job. Dom had given him one of his spare organic cotton white kaftans, so he did look the part, except for the blue ink stain on one of his hands.

To add a bit of credibility, Dom had told the driver that he sensed some healing capabilities within him, just to cover his bases.

The patient had lung cancer and had been prompted by the news slot to give the Haven a go. He was open to anything. He was asked to close his eyes and empty his mind. In the glint of candle light, Dom began the procedure by striking a tuning fork that sent a mid pitched hum around the room, it was the signal that the session was about to begin. It started with some low volume chanting in Latin, that translated in English to *be gone affliction*. Then, Dom placed his hand on the patient's forehead whilst the driver held the patients hands as per instructions. This part lasted for around five minutes. The speech then changed to English, though it wasn't clear what Dom was saying as he was muttering and speaking in whispers. That was the desired effect he was aiming for. There was no mention of God or Jesus, as was often the case in the so-called evangelical healers. The process was similar though, as Dom attempted to illicit a cure via mere thought and suggestion. His ultra white teeth were shining in the candle light. The whole process was over in around twenty minutes, then the lights were raised and the patient's relatives were allowed into the room. They helped him to his feet.

"I feel it went well." Dom said, "The mystic forces that work through me don't always give the outcome we desire, but I feel positive. Perhaps a second or third session would be of some benefit." The family members looked grateful. They helped their sick member out of the building, stopping at reception to make a *healthy* donation. Dom slipped two £20 notes into the hand of the delivery driver. "Remember not a word." The driver thought £40 for twenty minutes work was a lot more than he made delivering printer inks and A4 paper. Everyone was happy, except the patient, who still had cancer.

This was, in essence, why Dom had started the Haven and the whole project. The feeling that he had now was like no other; some tiny part of him thought he actually *had* some healing powers. Whatever the case, the endorphin rush he got from these sessions was worth all the baloney and...lies.

He strode the halls of the Haven more briskly after the fake healing sessions. He breezed past John, who was steadily buffering the floor without, for once, Pink Floyd pulsing through his earphones. John was usually pretty vacant in thought during this buffering process; he found it a form of meditation, with the music and the rhythmic whirr of the buffing machine. Today though, his mind was fully occupied with Andy's predicament and he felt a not insubstantial amount of guilt. Perhaps he had read the signs wrongly about Andy being the right person to pass the gift on to. It was what it was, however, and he hoped that a solution could soon be found.

# 29

Andy tried to take his mind off current events by watching the in-flight film, whatever the film was about was unknown as his mind continuously locked back onto the same subject. Eventually he gave up and just looked at the screen; it was a car chase and then some martial arts style fighting. Mick would have known what film it was.

This journey felt like a nightmare. If only he could've walked up to the cockpit and asked the pilot to step on the gas. It felt like a part of him was being dragged off somewhere else as he sat fidgeting in his seat. An immense feeling of inertia gripped him, but there was nothing he could about it except take it, second by second, minute by minute, hour by hour.

After enduring this torture for eight hours, the pilot announced that they would be landing at Lucknow in a matter of minutes; at least he could then get out of his seat and do something... take some kind of action. They landed at 6:30am

Indian time. The plane seemed to take forever to come to a complete halt. Andy passed through customs and immigration without issue and without the need to wait for cases, he headed outside to find a taxi. The humidity hit him like a wave and he was glad of the bottled water that John had given him. Even at 6:30 am, the airport was buzzing with a myriad of people scurrying around, each on their own personal mission. He called the number of the contact John had given him, it rang, but there was no response…perhaps it was a little too early. There were a million people in this city, not a massive number by India's standards, but still around the same size as Greater Manchester.

*How had he ended up here on this wild goose chase*? He had the phone number of someone and a landmark to head to and that was all. He pronounced *Hazratganj* to the best of his ability to the first available three wheeler taxi driver and the driver signaled for him to get in. The blue and green vehicle looked flimsy but was actually quite comfortable as it zipped around the frantic early morning traffic.

"Where exactly do you want sir?" the driver asked.

Andy was slightly surprised by his fluent English.

"The main market please."

"It's a big market, anywhere in particular?"

"Just the main entrance."

"Are you sightseeing?" the driver asked, as a matter of course. Lucknow did not generally attract British citizens, unless they had relatives there. The driver guessed by Andy's skin tone that he probably hadn't.

"Not exactly; I am looking for someone. Have you heard of Ramesh?"

The driver did not break his concentration, weaving in and out of the traffic. "Ramesh means *one that helps others.*" he informed. Andy didn't ask what the name meant.

"Do you know him?"

"I know some called Ramesh."

"He is also known as *the righteous one.*" Andy added.

"The righteous one." the driver repeated.

It hadn't previously occurred to Andy that the taxi drivers may have been a valuable source of information.

"Have you heard of him?"

"No, it rings a bell, maybe just a rumour." Andy's heart sank a little, "But it does ring a bell. Does he live near the market?" the driver asked, narrowly missing a man on a push-bike.

"I don't know, but that is where I am meeting the contact who knows him." Andy said.

"Oh, I see. Here is my card." The driver passed Andy a card with his number on it, "I will ask around. If you can't find him give me a ring, I may have found something out."

"Thank you. Thank you very much." Andy took the card and put it in his shirt pocket...there was a little more hope.

As the taxi drove through the city, Andy took in the wonderful buildings and sights with little interest, to him, at the moment, they were just in the way of his objective. Lucknow was a city on the up and had some considerable wealth though, like every city, it would have its less affluent side. According to John, Ramesh was not part of the wealthy side of town, that was if what Peter had remembered still held true. For all Andy knew, Ramesh may have been living in one of the expansive luxury apartments or mansions set in their own grounds that he saw passing by.

After about an hour, they arrived at the market. The driver brought the spluttering three-wheeler to a halt.

"Here we are." the driver said. Andy could see an ornate archway leading to the market. That was the supposed meeting place.

"Thanks. How much is it?"

The driver asked for four hundred rupees; around just five pounds sterling. The driver could have asked for four thousand rupees and Andy wouldn't have cared any less, just handed it over. Money, at present, was not an important object.

◆ ◆ ◆

He was now there in India, where he had imagined himself being less than twenty four hours ago. So far it was going to plan, but also, at the same time, he was no further forward in his objective than when he had left Manchester airport. He got out of the taxi, which with a spurt of smoke scurried off in the opposite direction.

There at the market entrance, there were more people, per square meter, than he could ever remember seeing. He got out his phone and called the number that John had given him on that piece of paper. This time there was no dial tone, not a lack of an answer, but no dial tone…it wasn't even trying to connect, as though the number didn't exist or the other phone had been turned off. Andy adjusted his wrist-watch to the local time and waited at the entrance, trying the number again every twenty minutes or so. Each time he got the same dead tone. He skipped through his options in his head…they were few. Either "a" he waited it out here to see if the guy turned up or had his phone turned on, or "b" ask around and try to find this healer as if he was a needle in a haystack. There was no "c".

He called John to tell him the updated news; John had his phone with him at work and had kept the music off so that he wouldn't miss a call. But, he had no answer as to why the mystery person from the forum was not connecting with Andy. Maybe he would later, or maybe the guy was just an internet troll who was making the whole *I was healed in India* story up, for whatever reason the trolls do what they do. If that was the case, then the whole trip would be fruitless. He advised Andy to wait another hour or two and see what happened. *What else could he do?*

At this point Andy should have been feeling hungry, but the knot in his stomach was overriding that. He had drunk both of the bottles of water he had brought with him and the humidity wasn't showing any signs of decreasing. It was almost like being in a sauna as it was unusually hot for the time of year. He was going to have to go into the bustling market and get more water. Perhaps it would be cooler in there. He did stand out as the only non-Indian man at the present time at the market, so if this elusive character turned up, Andy would be easy enough to spot in the crowd. He ventured inside.

He had to stick to the bottled water and preferably cooked western type food that he recognised. Some of the food on display might as well have been from another planet. *The never get ill* bonus of having the gift would probably have left along with the gift itself, so the last thing he needed was to be taken out of action with digestion problems. There were a multitude of stalls and some people with just a table of sorts in front of them, selling what looked like creatures or insects on sticks, along with different types of meat, plus a multitude of brightly coloured spices. Myriads of different types of fruit of all different colours, shapes and sizes, took centre stage at a lot of stalls. Andy bought some water and some fruit. Bananas seemed to be the only thing he felt able to eat at the moment, a banana was a banana, so there was no risk of the unknown. He bought two, along with an apple: carbohydrates to fuel him that did not need refrigerating. The bottled water was chugged down as if by a man lost in the desert. When he'd re-hydrated, he asked a stall holder if he knew someone that went by the name of Ramesh. The stall holder spoke only a little English, but did understand the question, he looked positive and gestured for Andy to walk down three stalls and then right two stalls. Andy hoped that this was a minor miracle; he followed the instructions, weaving in and out of the crowds of people, till he arrived at the stall in question.

"Ramesh?" Andy asked. An Indian man approximately in his late twenties took a step forward.

"Yes. Good day sir, what do you want? We sell many things here." he said, with a genuine smile. This definately did not look like the man in his seventies or eighties that John had told him about.

"I'm looking for Ramesh the healer. Is that you?"

"The healer? My name is the same, but healing is not something I offer here, sorry. Electrical goods, take a look, very good price." he said, still with the smile. Not only did this person not look like the Ramesh Andy was seeking....it obviously wasn't him.

"Do you know any other people called Ramesh?" Andy asked.

"Sorry no. Are you interested in a very cheap Iphone?" Andy moved on. This *was* going to be like searching for that proverbial needle. He decided to go back to the market entrance and re-group. *Where was the entrance?* He seemed to have gone off track and was lost in the middle of a sea of people. He headed in one direction and hoped eventually he would see his path back out. It was cooler in here than outside in the sunlight, but still very warm. He chugged more water and eventually, by sheer persistence, found the entrance. Perhaps the next time he ventured in there, he should lay string as Theseus had done in the maze. There was still no sign of the contact and still nothing from their phone. He chugged some more water. Then he remembered the card in his pocket with the taxi driver's number on it....by now he may have been able to find something out. He called the number and got a response; it was a little difficult to make out what the taxi-driver was saying amid the traffic noise in the background, but he said.

“Someone has heard of him, in that area. *A healer*, but that is all he would say, nothing more.” This wasn’t much but it *was* something in a sea of nothing. The taxi-driver would have no reason to make that up. Andy thanked him and looked skyward. He decided that the best plan now might be to ask as many other people as possible. He went back inside the market.

"Do you know Ramesh?" he asked repeatedly. Some market go-ers and stall holders answered, some didn't. The ones that did answer had nothing solid for him to use. He walked further in amongst the crowds of bustling people. The noise built up into a crescendo. His vision became blurry. There were too many people. He felt overwhelmed. Then he blacked out.

# 30

Jack had been staying with his gran for the last two days. He knew that Fran really wasn't well, as she was in hospital, and they scared him. He had been to one before and thought that the place smelled funny. On the tv, the hospital dramas he'd seen always seemed so serious, so *life and death.* He didn't want to go to the hospital, but he needed to see Fran and how she was doing, so he had asked his gran to take him with her. Mum was already there on a constant vigil.

When his gran arrived at the hospital car park, the building looked impossibly big to Jack and equally as intimidating. Once they were through the automatic doors and inside though, the maze of corridors were a source of amazement and the bustling friendly looking nurses were a bit more comforting. A ride in the talking lift, with its gleaming stainless steel was bordering on exciting and soon they were at the door to the separate room in the children's intensive care ward. Gran placed her hand on

Jack's shoulder as they entered. Jane went over to hug Jack as he tentatively walked over to the side of the hospital bed, where his sister was still in an induced coma. There were no signs of life: she wasn't moving, and her eyes were closed. The steady beep of the monitoring equipment was the only sign that she was still hanging in there. Jack looked at all the tubes and wires connected to Fran and he wanted to pull them all off, maybe they were the reason she wasn't well. It was distressful to him to see her like this, but he was glad that he had come and seen for himself.

His mother pulled him to her and wrapped her arms in front of him. They all just watched in silence for a while: helpless. All they could do was hope that the doctors and the NHS equipment could find the reason for her slow decline and do something about it. All this fancy complex machinery and they had so far come up with nothing, though not for the lack of trying.

Jack looked on and felt guilty. He had not felt even a little bit of regret about Rick dying. Perhaps he was being punished now by some unseen force.

"Is she going to wake up soon? Where is dad?" he asked his mother. She smiled at Jack, unable to answer the first question.

"He's coming as soon as he can." she replied. She wondered *where in hell are you Andy*?

◆ ◆ ◆

Five thousand miles away, Andy opened his eyes. He'd collapsed through exhaustion, stress, dehydration and whatever else that had contributed. Several market stall holders had picked him up off the ground and helped him into a comfortable postition; one of them was pointing an electric fan in his direction.

"Ok now?" the fruit seller smiled and nodded. Andy looked around and regained his bearings. He was sat at the back of a stall where he had enough room. Another stall holder passed him a bottle of spring water. Andy thanked him and took a healthy swig. He felt ok and remembered about plan “b”, *ask as many people as possible if they knew about Ramesh.*

The reason why the contact declined showing up or even answering his phone was unknown. Now all Andy could do was carry on asking. He got up and started walking around at a slower pace than previously. When some of the stall holders realized he was not about to buy anything they showed less interest; some that *could* speak English pretended that they couldn't. People were people, whichever country you were in. Some were more good natured and willing to help. He tried outside of the market, where the dust and traffic noise was equally as distracting as the rumbling murmur and echoed shouting inside. Plenty of people smiled at him, but no one had any useful information. He did not want to venture too far from the market entrance at first, but then realized that it seemed like a lost cause anyway, so he may as well try further afield. He ventured into some of the avenues around the market entrance; his feet seemed to carry him there of their own accord.

The sun began to hide behind clouds and before much longer the sky was overcast and dark grey: there was a storm brewing. Andy forced down a banana and and most of an apple just as the heavens opened and a flash rain storm hit. He took shelter under the canopy of a bar, the neon lights and dated architecture made it look like something from the sci-fi film *Blade Runner*. He ordered a beer whilst he was in there, repeating the question to the barman as he ordered.

"Sorry, I don't know this man." the barman said.  The beer was nice and cold. Andy took a seat on a bar stool and watched the rain pelting down off the roofs and ground outside. Lightning struck nearby...a wild fork of electricity. The raw power of nature. Another crack of lightning and a deep rumble seemed even nearer. He was going to have to sit this out. All he could do, for now, was wait and watch. Several minutes passed by.

"Intense is it not." A voice came from his left, Andy turned to see a slim, bald headed old man sitting near to him. He hadn't noticed him sit down. *Was he there before?* Andy smiled thinly and nodded, "Have you seen nature like this before? In India we have extremes like this. Monsoons, now *they* are something to behold."

"Not quite like this. We do get a lot of rain in Manchester." Andy said.

"Manchester, England. I like Manchester United. You seem troubled." the stranger said, "What troubles you? Not just the storm."

"You would not believe me if I told you." Andy replied.

"Perhaps I would."

"I'm looking for someone, I need their help and no one knows where he is. To be honest, I'm not sure he even exists."

"Who is this person you seek?"

"Ramesh, also known as *the righteous one*. I don't suppose you have heard of him?" Andy asked, not expecting a positive response.

"I *think* I have." the man said.

"Do you know him, or where he lives?" Andy became more animated and he sat up.

"Of a fashion."

"Do you know where I can find him? It's really important."

"He is close...you could say within touching distance."

"Touching distance, you mean not far?" Andy looked around the bar to see who else was in there. The man placed his hand on Andy's shoulder.

"I am the person you are seeking out." Andy looked both puzzled and amazed.

"You are Ramesh? How did you find me, or did I find you?"

"I felt you arrive, I was drawn to your aura, your essence."

"Out of so many people?"

"It was inevitable I would find you, something like two magnets attracting each other. Now, you have come all this way for a reason, have you not?"

"Yes, yes, a few days ago, I mean, something happened where I got this gift this..."

"You have corrupted your gift by using it selfishly, by letting your personal wishes and desires come into conflict with the reason you had been given the gift for."

"How did you know that?"

"And now you need to know if it can be *re-reversed* so to speak. So that you can once again come into contact with others. Possibly heal again. I gather you know that the reversal now means the gift causes harm instead of healing?"

"My daughter."

"Has she become ill?"

"Yes. Will she die?"

"That is unknown."

"How can I change what is happening?"

"It is not certain that you can."

"Look, I didn't come this far for you to answer in riddles. I need answers....please."

"You are receiving answers."

"Useful answers." Andy snapped.

"Patience."

"I don't mean to be rude, but I haven't exactly got all the time in the world. My daughter is dying and it's my fault."

"How deep are you willing to go?"

"What do you mean?"

"To what lengths will you go to try and reverse this?"

"Whatever it takes."

"Your own life?"

"If that's what it takes. Why would it take my own life?"

"Follow me; we will talk as we walk." Ramesh said and then they got up off the bar stools and stepped into the wet but rain free street that was already bustling again with people. Andy saw a light above this man's head, almost like a halo, it shimmered like the sun reflecting off a mirror, *or was it a trick of the light?*

"It's happened before then?" Andy asked. Ramesh nodded, "A lot of times?"

"Once or twice, that *I* know of. How many in total I cannot say." They kept walking at a brisk pace, Andy just a step behind this man who seemed surprisingly agile for someone that looked to be in his seventies.

"So how many have this gift, *in the world* I mean?"

"Just a handful."

"When did it all start, where does it come from?"

"We don't know exactly the origins."

"Thousands of years ago?"

"Yes, we know that." Ramesh said.

"Before Jesus?"

"Yes. Jesus was one, but a special one with the gift: he did not have to wait for a new dawn." Andy walked just behind and tried to digest that last statement. Before too long, they reached an urban area of very modest dwellings. Ramesh beckoned him inside his own house. "Please take a seat."

Inside were all the basics that you needed and not much more. Comfortable chairs and functional furniture. A kitchen was off the main room. There was an old jukebox in one corner, lit up and providing half of the light in the room. It looked like it came from the 1950's. This was no time for music.

"*Can* you do anything to reverse what has happened?" Andy asked, hopefully. The answer he got was not what he had wanted.

"No I cannot." Ramesh's facial expression did not change, "But *you* can. I can show you, but you must do it."

"What is it that I have to do?"

"A test."

"What kind of test?"

Ramesh sat down on the floor, cross legged.

"Tomorrow we shall rise before dawn."

"What then?"

"We will go somewhere known only to myself. There the test will take place."

"Where?"

"A cave."

"A cave?" Andy repeated.

"Yes, that is all you need to know for the present."

"Can't we go there now?"

"No. Just before dawn."

Andy looked carefully at this man who was giving off energy such as he had never felt before. They talked at some length, at a slow pace, whilst sipping strong tea.

"How long have *you* had this gift to heal?" Andy asked.

"More than sixty years. All told."

"Why have you kept the gift so long, if you don't mind me asking?"

"I gave it away once; it was the wrong thing to do."

"Why was that?"

"The person I gave it to was not worthy of it. I made a mistake. They tried to use it for their own personal gain."

"What happened?"

"It became reversed, became *the touch of death.*" Ramesh said and then he stared more deeply into Andy's very soul it seemed.

"The same as me." Andy said, flatly, "What did you do?"

"I tried to help him reverse it."

"How?"

"The same way *that we* are going to try just before dawn. The only way possible."

"What happened? Did it work?"

"It was not successful." Ramesh slowly shook his head.

"What happened to the..." Andy stopped mid question; from the look on Ramesh's face, he knew that the other person did not survive whatever this test was.

"He lived for only an hour after leaving the cave." Ramesh said, quietly.

"If you gave it away, does that mean you no longer have it?"

"It came back to me after it all went wrong. I do not know why it did that. Time is already getting on, get some rest, we rise very early." Ramesh tossed him a thin blanket.

"Can't you tell me any more?"

"Tomorrow."

◆ ◆ ◆

Andy woke up in the very early hours; he had slept through exhaustion, for how many hours he couldn’t say for sure. The air had been filled with a low urban drone until he could no longer keep his eyes open. Ramesh looked like he’d already been up and about for a while; if he ever slept in the first place.

“Almost time to go. Here, you need some strength for today.” He handed Andy a cup full of soup and a chunk of simple bread to go with it. Dawn was still a way off by the look of it; the night still as black as could be, with stars shining down clearly all across the sky. Ramesh went outside and strode purposefully across to a tarpaulin cover, which he removed to reveal a motorized scooter of some sort. He got on and then gestured to Andy to get onto the back of it. He turned the key and revved the tiny 50 cc engine, then without further ado, they set off. Slowly, steadily, they left the huddled together makeshift houses behind and before long they found themselves on a dirt track. It was so early and so surreal that Andy felt like he had completely lost touch with reality, almost like he wasn't really there at all. The bumps in the rough track helped jar him awake and back to the here and now. They rode along in silence, any words that either one said would have been drowned out by the high pitched engine. Time moved on and the sky became less black; the night air strangely sobering, particularly since neither rider had a helmet on. Andy became aware of the rythm of the puttering engine as, amidst the dust the bike was throwing up, all there was to see were trees, rocks and the stars.

After some time, Ramesh stopped the scooter next to a large rock. “Hang on.” he instructed Andy and then he turned the scooter away from the rough track, to no track at all... a totally unkempt route. He manoeuvred between rocks and shrubs and other natural obstacles, before turning again towards an assortment of larger rocks, illuminated only by the scooters headlight beam. He halted the scooter next to a particularly large rock. Andy could see nothing particularly special around, but Ramesh said. “We are here.” Then he produced a torch from a bag on the bike and instructed Andy to follow him. There was a hint that the sun was thinking about rising. Ramesh stopped still. He shone the torch on one particular area before moving some foliage and shrubs to one side. Revealed, was a natural opening in the rock, about a meter wide...the entrance to something.

“What’s in there?” Andy asked.

“The solution to your problem....perhaps.”

“Is that the cave you spoke of?”

“Yes. In there is a spring of liquid. It is a sacred place.”

“What do I have to do?” Andy asked. Ramesh’s

eyes were white in the star and moonlight.

"Simple, you must go inside and bathe your hands, your head and face in the waters of the spring."

"Will that reverse what has happened to me?"

"We will only know that afterwards."

"How does this work?"

"The spring runs through a sacred place. The place where life came. No one knows where it starts; no one knows where it ends. Some it has helped, some it has not."

*More riddles*. "What happened to the other ones it *didn't* help, besides the one you told me about?"

"Remember, I did say you would have to risk everything, like the others did." Ramesh said, his face more solemn, "Do you still want to go ahead? We can easily turn back if you wish."

"I have to. I have no choice."

"There is always a choice." Andy moved forwards with the intention to take the torch off Ramesh, for the darkness of the cave. "You will not need this." Ramesh said. Andy went to the cave entrance; sure enough, inside there was a soft glow of light, "Bathe but do not drink from the spring. Good luck." Andy looked back at him briefly before ducking down and entering the cave, "I cannot follow you, my energy may affect the result. You have to go in there alone." Ramesh called as Andy entered.

Inside the cave, there was a very dim glow that became slightly brighter when he entered, *or was that his imagination.* He was aware of many crystals in the roof of the cave that were giving off a faint but distinctive glow that was just enough to see by. There was no sound in the cave other than the gentle, constant trickle of water which was breaking free of the rock briefly, before heading out of sight again. The water shimmered in the light of the crystallized rock, sometimes looking blue, then silver then effortlessly becoming other colours. Andy knelt down in front of the spring. *There is always a choice* Ramesh had said. *This water is the key*? *This thin stream of translucent water coming out of an ordinary looking rock in a non-descript cave.* It seemed too easy and too simple. Then he stopped. There was another separate stream further along. Ramesh had not said anything about *two* streams. Perhaps he didn't know. Andy took a breath and tried to clear his mind in order to choose, or was he supposed to bathe in both? He steadied himself and then went over to the stream further back in the cave. The water in this stream seemed to dance and flicker. He made his choice, crouched down and placed his hands under the stream; it's natural flow was disturbed and it continued on to its destination through the gaps in his fingers. He cupped his hands together and let the water flow over his head, and then he bathed his face as Ramesh had said he should. He lowered his hands, having fulfilled Ramesh's instructions. He got back to his feet, feeling no immediate change. *Was this for real or pure fantasy?* Then he remembered there was no such thing as *fantasy* any longer: his experience with the gift had expelled any meaning to that word. He left the cave and rejoined Ramesh at the entrance.

"You did the things I mentioned?" Ramesh asked.

"Yes."

"You drank from the spring also?"

"No. Was I supposed to? There were two streams."

Ramesh shook is head. Actually, he was not completely sure about the consequances of drinking the from the stream. He looked at Andy more intently, as though, once again, staring into his very soul. At one time this would have unnerved Andy, but not now, "How will I know if I have passed the test?"

"There is one good sign." Ramesh said.

"What's that?"

"You were able to leave the cave. You were not incapacitated."

"I suppose that is good."

"Do you want to know now?"

"If you can tell me."

Ramesh took a small knife from a pouch on the scooter; slowly he drew the knife across the thumb of his left hand. He wiped the blade and returned it to the pouch. Blood dripped from the two inch wound on to the dusty ground. "Try to heal me."

"But what if it has *not* worked and I make you ill?"

"I can cut, but I cannot get ill." stated Ramesh. Andy took a deep breath and two steps to be within touching distance. Looking only at Ramesh's hand, he slowly outstretched his own hand until his fingers make contact for five seconds. Then he pulled his hand slowly back. Nothing was said for one long minute. The thumb was still bleeding. No change.

"It's not worked." sighed Andy, "What happens now, can I try it again? There were two streams, perhaps I chose the wrong one."

"You chose and then followed the steps?" Ramesh asked.

"Yes."

"Then there is no point. A second time may be fatal, as it was the other time. There is great power at work here."

"This is the right cave?" Andy asked.

"Yes. The power of the stream is not in doubt." Ramesh placed his hand on Andy's shoulder, "Do you feel ok?" Andy nodded, "Then with luck, we have not made things worse."

They returned to the scooter and began the journey back. The sun was just beginning to break the horizon, a new day was breaking and all the possibilities of a brand new day lay ahead. The night creatures were retreating back to their hiding places, birds began to chirp their dawn chorus and the day time creatures began to rouse themselves. Andy felt disconnected from all of it. Waves of hopelessness and emptiness pulsated over him. *What on earth was he going to do now?*

Ramesh kept the pace of the scooter even; methodically swerving bigger stones on the track. When he got to the point where they had turned off the beaten track he stopped briefly and swept away the tyre tracks with a branch from a bush, removing any trace of the route that they had taken.

When they arrived back at his home, it was just about daylight. They walked inside in silence. Ramesh wrapped a makeshift bandage around the two inch gash on his thumb, and then he passed a bottle of water to Andy.

“That’s it then.” Andy said. Ramesh did not reply, but took a ragged looking book off an old bookshelf; he began reading certain parts, flicking through pages, before placing it back on the shelf, “Wait, why didn't I think of this before, you could come to England with me! You still have the power to heal.” Andy said. Ramesh looked right at Andy without expression.

“I cannot, I am sorry. I have to stay here.”

“I will pay for your ticket and everything.”

Andy pleaded.

"I have to stay here. Regardless, I have no passport. I am very sorry."

"Can you pass your gift onto me? I can return it back to you after I have used it to heal my daughter?"

"I swore I would never again pass on the gift after the last time, I cannot go back on that now. I am sorry."

# 31

At the Haven, Dom was tip tapping on his desk with his fingers as he looked at the screen. He was reviewing footage from the Haven's CCTV cameras. A time consuming process and patience definitely not being one of his virtues, it irritated him that he couldn't delegate this task. He pressed pause on the replay to freeze the frame on an image of the new chef placing his hand on a patient in the dining room. *Kinney, Grace Kinney*, he mouthed to himself. He checked his office computer on an adjacent screen and found the datbase record for Grace Kinney. It listed her as *cancer treatment...now in remission*, dated two weeks ago.

He moved on from Grace and continued to check footage; trying to map out the successful treatments of patients to images of their contact with this new chef, or anyone else for that matter. He wrote anything that cross referenced down in a small notebook: he didn't want a digital record of what his findings amounted to.

A *tick* signified it had been checked and verified by footage. When he took a break, he closed the book and then looked up at some of the images and certificates on his office walls. Some of them related to the machines he had been credited with developing; others his qualifications. Then there were photographs of himself standing next to some of the cured patients. At the very front was one of him holding a giant oversized cheque that he was giving to charity. A call came through to his office from his secretary.

"Mr Leach is here to see you Dominic." Penny said. Dom was even more irritated by the interruption.

"About what? I am quite busy."

"He is here from the WMA consortium."

Dom perked up at that news and closed down the footage, for now. Impolitely, he asked Penny to send up Mr Leach, the representative of the large conglomerate, and then he watched him through the active CCTV as he made his way up to Dom's office, flicking from one camera to the next, giving Dom the perfect timing to open his white office door at the precise moment Leach was about to knock. With his slightly sardonic smile in place, he ushered his guest in, before sitting back casually in his plush office chair. He surveyed Leach with an air of detachment, intended to give Leach the impression he was doing him a favour by doing business with him.

Leach opened with a slightly uncomfortable cough; he'd been in the medicine and health industry for the last twenty years and was far from convinced that these alternative therapy machines actually worked, even though the numbers said that they did in black and white. Every so often in the industry there were *fads*, as Leach saw them, most of which faded into the background like one hit wonders in music. Methods that claimed to revolutionize a particular area of medicine; or some *miracle* drug that seemed to be an answer to a problem, but the testing data has been misleading, or simply fabricated. He had been one of the initial doubters on the Theranos blood testing scandal. He hadn't trusted its founder from day one. Leach remained ever sceptical; he wanted to see the results of the successful treatments and then some more. Oscillating crystals just don't cut it for him, but his bosses invested in cold hard data; like a football manager signing a player they may or may not specifically like, but who scores twenty five goals *every* season.

"It is remarkable what you say these machines can achieve Dominic." Leach said. He was thinking about Elizabeth Holmes, the founder of the bogus and elaborate Theranos blood test con, as he said it. Dom was slightly perturbed that Leach was ok with using his first name.

"Thank you Mr. Leach, can I call you Ryan?

It's all true, we have all the figures carefully documented, obviously." Dom handed Leach a folder with the necessary data to back up his claims. Leach poured over the figures as though he had only just seen them, in truth, he had already poured meticulously over this information for the last two days. He checked to see if the printouts he had received earlier may have been flawed. They looked the same.

"How many of these crystal machines do you have at the Haven?"

"Three…at present."

"Do you intend to produce more? I mean, even if say, we did *not* decide to back your expansion."

"Oh yes, their success rates cannot be overlooked. We will produce more and ultimately, open more clinics, such as this one. To be honest, we *will* do this with or without the WMA's backing, it would just take a little longer. I feel a certain responsibility to the public and also to the world of medicine not to stop at just this single place."

"But do you intend to sell the machines, both types, if the right offer came in? Possibly creating a franchise?"

"Like KFC you mean? My machine's workings are a secret after all, just like the recipe." Dom chuckled at his own joke, "Yes, we will sell them, at a fair price, I want to help as many people as possible and if we can be rewarded for our endeavours then I don't think anyone could begrudge that."

Leach instinctively saw the man across the desk as a pure business man, just like so many others he had encountered, and not some *hero*. He was not fooled by everything that came out of Dom's mouth. He was still thinking about Theranos and its peircing eye'd founder.

"Aren't you currently registered as a charity?" Leach asked.

"Yes." Dom answered, flatly.

"Forgive me for asking, but what or who pays for all this, so far I mean?"

Dom sat back in his chair. "We do have some wealthy and *grateful* users of the facility, oh and not to forget the important lottery funding."

"You have Lottery funding? That is not easy to get. Why not just simply sell the machines to the highest bidders then?"

"I would prefer to make sure that they are used properly. My position is such that I would prefer to concentrate on the equipment and treatments and let another party, such as your good selves, the people that you represent, come in with the backing. Underwrite the whole venture. Then I can concentrate on what I do best."

"Which is?"

"Healing people...of course."

"The Conglomerate I represent, the WMA,

became so huge by taking several calculated chances. Always based on good foundations and hard facts, you understand."

"I understand. That is why I have the figures in such detail for you. It's all in black and white, these machines work. Not 100% of the time, granted, but the statistics show a greater than 50% cure in illnesses unsuitable for other treatments."

"I've seen the figures." Leach said, nodding. Then, changing tone slightly, "My superiors would like a demonstration, before they write the cheque for £150 million."

"Please, no one writes cheques any more, do they?" Dom laughed.

"I suppose I was speaking figuratively. They would like to send four patients over the next two weeks. If two of them, at *least* two of them, are cured, in time of course, then they will provide the relevant investment and backing."

"Which patients?" Dom asked.

"They are going to be specifically selected by the company. How do you feel about this?" Dom did not like being made to jump through hoops, not at all, but he saw no problem in the request and they would have to eat even more humble pie when the results of this test were positive. "They want to be certain; think of it as an independent trial."

"I have no problem with that. When do you

intend to start this trial?" Dom asked.

"In the next few days, if that is ok with you? They may already have patients in mind." Dom rose from his chair and Leach did likewise. They shared an unconvincing handshake, "I'm sure you are very busy, I'll be in touch soon. I can find my own way out." Leach said. Dom showed him to the door and they said their goodbyes. He watched Leach leave on the CCTV.

This Leach person was someone that he hadn't run rings around and been able to convince with his charm alone. Dom would have the last word though and it would taste sweeter when it happened. He buzzed down to his assistant, more politely this time. "Penny, when is the new chef, what's he called again? Back at work? See if you can get hold of him as soon as you can, would you please. I need to speak urgently with him." He ended the call and then stared out of his office window into the Haven's lush and expansive grounds. He had known what was happening with John and had taken the attitude, *if it isn't broke, don't fix it.* Now there was a spanner in the works. He had never imagined that this, what he thought was a completely *unique* power, could also belong to someone else.

◆ ◆ ◆

Two miles away, in the intensive care

department of the hospital, Jane was talking to the doctor. Grim faced, he was shaking his head. Jane had asked if they had discovered yet what was wrong with Fran, but her symptoms had no cause that they could detect. It was not a virus or any other recognosed or documented illness and that wasn't just his own opinion, every other leading physician he had contacted said the same thing. He had never seen a case like this before, neither had anyone else. It was almost as though her body was shutting down for no reason.

"Is her condition worsening?" Jane asked. The doctor nodded.

"Very slowly." he said. Jane looked at the equipment in the room and for all the advanced technology on show, it wasn't one jot of help, "Her decline is slowed by the induced coma." the doctor said, "I'm sorry to say this, but we don't know how long she has unless we can find out what the cause is. We can't try to treat her until we know what the problem is."

Jane felt this must just be a bad dream. Perhaps the whole of last few months had been. Sometime soon she may wake up and Fran would be there running around as usual.

"Is she going to…?" She couldn't bring herself to say the word; it would not form on her lips. The doctor had confronted this conversation many times over the years, it never got any easier.

"She may not have too long. I'm so sorry, but

you may have to prepare yourself for the worst." he said. Jane wept; she thought she was all cried out. When she recovered her composure a little, she got her phone out and called Andy's number, the tone sounded a little different, but he did answer.

"Where are you? You need to come now." she said. Andy was standing outside of Ramesh's home.

"How is she?" he asked. Jane told him that Fran was slowly getting worse and repeated to him the doctor's warning.

"You need to get here right now." she stressed. Andy paused for a second, the helplessness of his situation almost overwhelming him like a huge wave crashing into a solitary boat in the ocean.

"I can't get there right away."

"Why not, where are you?"

Andy sighed. "I'm in India."

"India, did you just say India?"

"Yes."

"What the hell are you doing in India, with Fran like this, are you totally stupid? You need to be here!"

"I can't explain right now, but I'm coming back on the next available flight." Jane ended the call in disgust. Andy felt like all his sins had come home to roost at once; he looked across at Ramesh who was looking back at him with both concern and inappropiate seeming tranquillity.

“I have to go back as soon as I can.” Andy said. Ramesh said nothing in reply, but went over to his weathered looking laptop and checked on the available flights back to the UK. After a short time he said.

“There is one flight leaving in four hours. Some seats are left…do you want me to book it?” Andy nodded, “I will take you to the airport. How are you for money?”

“Ok.” Andy said. Ramesh finished booking the flight, and then closed the lid on his laptop.

“We will need to set off within the hour.”

◆ ◆ ◆

The scooter was soon weaving its way through obstacles once again, though this time it was other traffic, not rocks and shrubs. In normal circumstances, Andy might have wondered how all these different vehicles could dart in and out of each other, seemingly with no rules, without having constant collisions. It was like a video game on the hardest difficulty setting. Ramesh's reflexes were still as sharp as a tack for an eighty year old. The mood on this journey was even more solemn than the trip to the cave: at least at that time there was some hope. It seemed he wasn’t worthy of having the healing power restored, some higher, unseen, unforgiving power had decided. It also seemed devastatingly unfair that Fran was suffering the repercussions of his mistake.

Eventually, minor crashes avoided, the scooter arrived at the airport; they dismounted and brushed the dust off themselves. Ramesh took the glove off his left hand, the cut was still there and it dripped a defiant single drop of blood.

“You have an hour before departure….I am truly sorry how things are.” Ramesh said. Andy couldn't seem to respond and form his own words, “You can call me  at any time, night or day.” Ramesh continued. Andy managed to say *thank you* and he gave Ramesh a light embrace, before turning and walking towards the airport's entrance doors. Ramesh stood and watched for a time, before getting back on the scooter and heading off back home. Andy looked up at the sign, *Lucknow Airport,* in several languages. *Luck* seemed to be conspicuous by its absence. He was too numb to see the irony, as he went through the motions of checking in and boarding the plane like a robot. As he waited to get on the plane , he wondered. *When John had seen the light around him that first day, had he been mistaken?* Whatever the answer was, he hadn’t asked for this power....less of a gift more like a curse. Something cruel that was waiting for him to slip up, make a mistake, so that he could then be punished in the most destructive way. He *had* chosen not to help Rick, but that decision still did not feel wrong...not in his heart anyway. *Would he do the same thing again?* That man, Rick, was not a good person. That said, had he, Andy, the right to be judge and executioner? He certainly was paying the ultimate price for that decision, or more accurately, Fran was. *Would he ever see her alive again?*

The flight attendant gave her well practiced safety drill and before long the plane took off. There was not the same urgency on this return trip: his reason for coming here had drawn from an empty well. He was returning empty *handed*.

This time, Andy was in the middle of two other passengers. He closed his eyes, having not slept much. In his mind he replayed the strange events of the last few days and above all else he wished that he had never been chosen... everything was simpler before that day, not good in many ways, but not *disastrous* like this. He may not have seen his kids much after the proposed move, but at least they would be alive and well, *somewhere*. Somehow, he drifted off into a turbulent, troubled sleep.

# 32

Dom checked himself in the mirror. He had to look the part...look a certain way. If he looked a certain way, then the acting would be a little easier, the mask easier to maintain. He had a degree in psychology; the certificate was proudly on his office wall. That proved his intelligence: he wasn't able to buy the certificate, like he could with most things. He had studied personality disorders, and the so-called *cluster b* group, which included narcissists, sociopaths and psychopaths. Narcissistic personality disorder or NPD for short, described an individual who very often had, amongst other things, a lack of empathy towards others. There was of course a spectrum, as with many disorders, and some people had a *complete* lack of empathy, others just little less than the average person. Some sufferers of NPD had *complete* grandiose delusions, some just a little. Sociopaths cranked things up another notch. Psychopaths were the worst flavour of the cluster b family and it is believed by many professionals that they were born, not made. Did Dom recognise any  of the traits of a cluster b disorder within himself? No. Perhaps he did in his sub-conscious. He remembered he had quite an abusive father and a difficult childhood, but he had risen above those dark days to become a complete success. In fact, that difficult start in life had made him a better person, or so his inner voice told him. His *other* voice, the one based on reality, didn't get any airtime.

There was a polite knock on his office door, he opened it. John was standing there feeling quite curious as he'd never before been called in to see Dom in his office in all the time that he had been at the Haven.

"Come in John. Take a seat. You know I've never had the chance to really speak with you. That's bad on my part, I should make more time to get to know my staff. How long have you been here now?"

"Five years Mr..."

Dom interrupted. "Please, no *Mr*, call me Dom. You must like it here then I hope, otherwise you wouldn't have stayed." Dom said with a smile.

"Yes, I suppose I must."

"Do you have a wife and kids?"

"I had a wife; the kids are grown up now."

"John, I hear you are thinking of hanging up the old mop and retiring soon. And I think it is time we rewarded you for all your hard work and loyalty. I think an increase in salary is in order....backdated." John looked pleased as most cleaners were on minimum rate, himself included. But then he got the feeling that this generous offer was not coming from the goodness of Dom's heart: he most probably wanted something in return, "I'm going to double your hourly rate." John looked more surprised and thought that his suspicions about Dom wanting something in return may have been well placed.

"Double?" he asked.

"Yes, your *calibre* of work is very rare. You see, I think you have brought more to the Haven than just polished floors, although you do that task very well."

"I don't exactly follow you...Dom." He obviously did know where Dom was heading but tried not to let it show on his face.

"To be blunt John, I'm hoping you will stay on at the Haven a while longer. How about if we *treble* your rate?" He paused for a few seconds to see if John reacted favourably to that offer. He got no indication. He cut to the chase, "Would you consider yourself to have anything *special*?"

"Special?"

"Have you heard of *John of God*? Coincidently you share the same name." Dom said.

"Is he a faith-healer in America?"

"South America. He has, supposedly, the

power to heal. Many people think it is all complete nonsense. I'm only guessing that you are not one of those people."

"I'm quite open-minded, but I've never really thought about it." John said. He was an unconvincing liar.

"I believe he *does* have healing powers, I also believe he is not the only one who has them."

"I see."

"Do you know where I am going with this John?"

"I'm not totally sure."

Dom sat even further back in his chair. "It took me a while, but what you have to remember is that we have cameras in abundance here at the Haven, for security reasons. John, I looked at the patients who made a recovery whilst having treatment here, some very ill people that made a *complete* recovery...*miraculous* recovery. One's which John of God himself would be proud of. And there is always one common denominator."

"The machines?" offered John.

"Not just the machines. Take a look at this." Dom turned the CCTV playback screen so that John could see it. It showed John removing a glove and touching a patient on the arm. He freezed the specific frame, "This is just one example of many, from about a month ago I believe. The footage is kept for three months before being overwritten. This patient, like in all the other examples, made a complete recovery, almost immediately. I think that you, John, have a *gift*." John saw something akin to a reptilian expression flash across Dom's face for a split second, as though a sharp forked tongue might dart out at any second.

"I don't know what to say."

"Well don't say anything for the moment. But it does seem like you have taken a back seat recently, in terms of the healings." Dom tried to feign empathy, "What really intrigues me John is whether you had this gift before you came here and whether or not that was the *reason* why you came here?" John, no longer having the gift, found it a lot harder to read people. Since he passed it on to Andy, everything and everybody seemed more *veiled*. He waited for a few moments and scanned the ornaments and objects placed around Dom's office, hoping that some inspiration on how to respond might come to him. It didn't manifest itself. Dom, detached as always, used his non verbal skills to try and read John, who had yet to answer the question, "Do you still have the power to heal people?" Dom asked.

"No."

"You did have it though?" John felt it would be wrong to lie and knew he was bad at it anyway, so he opted to say nothing. Dom smiled once again, "I suppose the fact that you are not denying it means that you did. Please believe me John, your secret is safe and there is absolutely nothing to be concerned about. This is not an interrogation after all. I am not trying to trick you." John remembered all those years ago when his own mentor, Peter, had passed the gift on to him. He had stressed that it was best to keep it a secret, to avoid those that might want to use it and manipulate it. Keep it simple and uncomplicated. But he couldn't deny it, to lie would have felt wrong and, again, he was a terrible liar...always had been. Dom turned the screen back. "You could continue to be an invaluable asset John; I mean for doing good on a wider scale. We *are* looking to expand." Dom turned the screen around to show more footage, this time of Andy placing his hand on one of the patients, "This patient also made a recovery very soon afterwards; in fact they were discharged the very next day. This is no coincidence I'm sure. Please don't think I am trying to make you feel uncomfortable, believe me I'm not. I just think that you could do more with this gift you have."

"I don't have a gift."

"Do you mean, *any longer*? Did you pass it on somehow to the new chef, Andrew?"

John pursed his lips, he surmised that a lack of response was going to be as good as a *yes*, but he wouldn't lie about it. "Look Mr Pearce... Dom, I really do have a lot to be getting on with." Dom switched off the CCTV playback and folded his arms across his chest. He hated it when people didn't fully comply with his wishes; he manifested that with another sardonic smile.

"Of course John, I thank you for your time. Check your bank account; I think your loyalty and service to the Haven more than deserves a bonus."

John got up and left the office, unsure of how well he just handled the meeting. He knew he found it harder to read people lately, and he felt like he had been manipulated but couldn't quite put his finger on *how* exactly. I mean, it had just been a few questions and he hadn't *really* been pressured into answering any of them.

He would need to speak to Andy as soon as he returned to give him the heads up. With that idea in mind, he returned to the corridor and the buffer machine. He had felt a sense of relief since passing on the gift to Andy, what he hadn't told Andy is that it was in no way set in stone that he'd had to pass it on to someone else, ever. He could have kept it, just like Ramesh in India had. In truth, he had grown weary of the responsibility; he wanted a nice quiet life in retirement, a small boat, a fishing rod, a couple of beers at the weekend kind of retirement that was now within touching distance. Dominic had thrown *another* spanner in the works, on top of the disaster of Andy's gift reversal. *Had he made a terrible mistake in choosing Andy in the first place?* It *was* a hasty decision. He hoped and prayed that everything would be resolved on Andy's return. He said another prayer and flipped the switch on the buffer machine. No music this time.

# 33

On the plane, Andy's eyes opened slowly. He had been dreaming, but he didn't remember the dream, just the feeling it left behind. Next to him on his right, in the window seat, was an overweight man in his fifties, his hand was methodically delivering peanuts to his mouth with a robotic efficiency. To his left was a thin Indian man in his early twenties, dressed in an expensive looking suit, tapping away on what looked like the latest version of the I phone. He was tapping with a similar regularity and rhythm as the hand to his right with the peanuts. Andy checked his phone; no messages for two hours. It displayed only 2% battery charge left; he didn't know it but had lost the charger when he collapsed in the market. There was a charging port in front of him and he looked for the phone charger lead in the small bag he had as hand luggage. Not there. *It can wait* he thought. An hour passed by. The man to his right had finished with the nuts and had moved on to some kind of chewy sweets, Andy knew they were chewy by the constant motion of the man's jaw; he was watching the in-flight film as though he was at the cinema.

Then Andy's phone vibrated with a text message alert, but the effort to vibrate seemed to have used the last of its charge and the screen went black. He didn't have a charging lead, but had a strong need to read the message. He looked at the man with the sweets, then the man to his left and decided that he was the better option to ask first. Andy tapped him lightly on the shoulder and he turned without expression.

"I am sorry to disturb you; please do you have a lead I could borrow? I can't find mine to charge my phone." The man said nothing, did not even remove his headphones, but took a quick look at Andy's phone and then produced a USB cable from his bag and gave it to him. Andy thanked him and plugged it in to the port. Within a few minutes it displayed 3%, and he switched it on. When the screen came to life, it reported one new message, from Ramesh. Only a few words with a photo. Andy got out his reading glasses, which fortunately he still had with him: the text seemed smaller than usual for some reason, maybe it was his fatigue. It took a second to register the fact that Ramesh had sent as photo of his left thumb, the one he cut with a knife hours earlier. The cut had gone. The text read simply, *it worked.* Andy processed this information slowly. *Was he still dreaming*? No, he *was* awake, the cut had gone. The ritual in the cave had worked; it had just taken longer than they had expected. A rush of adrenaline kicked into his system, *all was not lost*.

The fear of not getting back to Fran in time suddenly magnified, and it supplanted the fear of losing her and filled its space equally. He was about halfway through the journey back, more or less, and now he would need another big slice of good fortune, but perhaps the tide was turning. He sat back in his seat and rested his head against the headrest. He pictured his daughter in the hospital; he was still so far away but getting closer with every passing minute.

Another hour passed, the guy to his right had run out of food and was dozing. The man to his left had ceased his feverish activity and was just letting time pass. Then, out of the blue, there was a little commotion up ahead, around ten rows up, flight attendants were buzzing around intently. Some of the passengers were murmuring. One of the flight attendants appeared with what looked like an oxygen mask. They appeared calm, not frantic, but were moving swiftly as though following some well rehearsed procedure. Andy couldn't tell what was happening, when suddenly one crew member asked.

"Is there a doctor on board please?" Then, after getting no response, she repeated the request. It must have been something fairly serious for them to ask for a doctor. Twelve rows ahead, a lady in her sixties was having real trouble breathing and had moved into a dangerous place; her face was tinted with blue. No-one on board responded to the doctor request. Andy knew, though not a doctor, he was able to help this woman now that he had the power back, but he also knew that if he did it would use up his dawn till dusk healing allowance. He had healed Ramesh before dawn so that counted as the previous day. But, crucially, if he helped this person, then the chance to help Fran would be put back to the next day...the next dawn. The scenario of many options and effects and causes flashed through his mind in a second. He begged fate for a doctor to stand up... they didn't. Andy stood up.

"Yes." he said. The man to his left looked surprised, but swiftly moved to let Andy past. Andy had no medical training, of course, and would have been better suited to providing the in-flight meal. He moved down the centre aisle, the crew looking at him with a sense of relief, and the responsibility had been largely taken off their shoulders. Andy saw the Lady. To him she looked approximately seventy years old...a decent of length life. In terms of number of years lived, that was decent. Fran was just starting out in life. The scales didn't balance if he healed this lady and wasn't able to heal Fran because of it. He had to block that thought out, what he had learned, to his cost, was that he had to do what felt right, not what he wanted. *Not* saving this woman's life, if he could, was not right. *If he did the unselfish thing, surely everything would work out.*

"She's not breathing properly." The flight attendant said quietly to Andy, he darted a look at the companion of the lady in trouble, *possibly her daughter?* The colour had drained out of her face, and she was trembling with panic. Meanwhile, another crew member had gotten the defibrillator and was beginning the procedure. Andy watched closely what she did with the pads. There was no response from the lady in trouble. Andy realized he needed to make contact and soon. He touched the woman's forehead as though he was checking her temperature. Then he took the pads off the crew member and tried the defibrillator again, only knowing how to use it from watching the first attempt. Suddenly, the woman drew a breath of air, then another and before long her breathing steadied.

"Was she ill before she got on the plane?" he asked the woman's companion.

"She has bad asthma. That's all I know." she replied. Andy held the lady's wrist to check her pulse, trying to look authentic.

"She seems stable now. Take her to be checked out after we land as a precaution. This kind of thing can be an indicator of heart problems." Andy said. Somehow he knew her heart was the problem, or at least it was five minutes ago.

Andy was thanked by the crew and the daughter. Some of the other passengers clapped in approval. The lady seemed to have been healed immediately, as it was before, so that was back to *normal.* Ramesh's thumb had taken longer for some reason, perhaps whilst nature or whatever it was that was behind this power had made its decision on what to do with him. Now all he had to do was get back to Fran and wait for the new dawn.

◆ ◆ ◆

The plane landed right on schedule and the passengers filed off down the stairway in an orderly fashion. Andy resisted the temptation to tell them all to hurry up. Halfway down the stairs he had a thought, *what if it was the defibrillator that had brought the woman back from the brink, rather than him?* He put an extra spring in his step, just in case he hadn't used up his daily *lifeline,* as he had started to think of them. Getting to the hospital as soon as possible was the priority. It was 4:00 pm UK time, just over fourteen hours till the new dawn. *Who or what was monitoring these timescales?*

The queue at immigration control was long.

He hoped to god that security didn't stop him, they hadn't stopped anyone so far. He had no cases to collect, so it should've been fairly straight forward. *Did he have his face set right? Did he look suspicious?* Was trying not to look suspicious actually making him look guilty of something? *Oh God, of all days don't stop me now*.

"Anything to declare sir?" They asked him. He was looking dishevelled, in yesterdays clothes and still grubby from crawling around in the cave and the dust.

"No." he answered. They checked his passport.

"Have a good day sir." They said. He was through. All he needed to do now was to jump in a taxi. First though, he had to draw out some money from the cash machine. The taxi would not accept rupees, which was all he had in his pockets. Looking as he did, like a homeless person, they would probably want to see some evidence of the fare. Out of three machines, one was free. *Things were going smoothly*. He put his bank card in; funds had been hit by the flight costs, but he still had the money John had transferred to him. Things had been so chaotic the last few days, Andy had to stop and think what his PIN number was. He remembered it just after the machine sucked in the card. There was some whirring noise from the machine, it was taking a while, *or was that how long it normally took?* Then there was an error message on the screen. *Error please contact your local branch.* Andy pressed every button available, more than once, he even resorted to using his fist, to the amusement of a nearby child. The damn thing wouldn't give him any money *or* his card back; this had happened to him before, but the machine had spat his card back out at him in disgust. This time it was keeping it, *or would it spit it out again after he had gone?* He hit it again. Still the same message on the screen; then, after looking down, he saw a piece of card on the ground, he picked it up...on the side that was facing downwards, it said *Do not use! Out of order awaiting repair Please use another machine.* That was all well and good advice, except that he couldn't use another machine as the broken one had spitefully kept his card. All he could do now was cash in the rupees at the exchange booth and hope for the best.

There was a queue and also some infernal woman in front of him with a big bag of coins, but eventually, the laid back man in the booth was asking what he would like and he was pulling all the Indian currency out of his pockets in notes and coins. It turned out to be £26.67 in pounds and pence.

"Thanks." Andy said and then he headed outside for a taxi.

"I've got £26 and the rest when we get there." he said to the first driver.

"Sorry, no can do. I'm booked." was his reply.

To the driver, Andy looked a little suspicious... grubby with no luggage. He'd had more than one *runner* this week. The second taxi driver was a little more chilled and took the risk that this passenger wasn't a runner; whatever he looked like.

"Ok, get in. Where to?"

Andy told him his home address, which was actually on the way to the hospital. He wasn't sure if he had enough to cover the fare at home, but would worry about that later. The taxi was old and well used, its diesel engine roared into life and it clunked into gear.

Before long they were on the motorway. Andy watched the white lines flash by in rhythmic fashion. Cars cruising by on the opposite side, cars flying past the taxi, exceeding the speed limit. People rushing to meet loved ones, travelling from work or whatever they were going, each had their own story. Not one of them in the same situation he was in. It was in fate's hands now whether or not he got there on time. *Twelve hours to the new dawn.* Andy was so tired that much of his capacity for rational thought was diminished. He closed his eyes to the rhythm of the tyres on the bumps on motorway tarmac and the dull thud as the taxi passed over chevrons. He drifted off, not into sleep, but a semi-conscious state, where the immediate dramatic state of events faded into the background. He snapped out of it when the driver turned up the radio a little as a song he liked came on. The brief respite had sharpened his senses a little. The motorway signs told him he was around twenty minutes away; he clenched his fist with a quiet resolve.

# 34

John had been thinking for quite a while about what type of boat he could get when he retired. He had checked his bank balance and, sure enough, there was a *bonus* payment, a bonus of several years salary in one go. The Haven wasn't clean enough to warrant *that*; he knew that it was a bribe in order to either illicit more information on the gift, or influence the situation to Dom's advantage some other way. With this bonus, the length of his boat could increase by six, eight, ten feet or even more. He didn't feel as though he had *accepted* a bribe, it was just there, on the screen of his laptop. The paid in column read £1209.41 each month and then a garish looking £43.000. Why Dom hadn't rounded it up to 50,000 was a mystery to John, but it came, not from the Haven, but from a property company. Perhaps an uneven number like *43* was less obvious than *50* if someone were to check through that company's accounts. Whatever the reason, it was a huge amount of money to someone like John, who throughout his life had always been making ends meet on a low income. John would not have accepted the money if handed it in cash, but there it was, already in his account. He had not seen the notes or even a cheque; it was *just* numbers in black and white on the screen. The more he looked at it didn't make it sit any easier. Was it payment for healing all the people he already had at the Haven or things that he was now expected to do...information he was now expected to now give?

So far he hadn't actually given anything concrete, but Dom did not strike John as the kind of person that gave without receiving. The truth about the healings, Dom had seemed to figure out on his own...with the help of the CCTV footage. *Was that money just a payoff to keep him quiet? For him to forget the conversation in the office took place? Or was it for something else?* John got the feeling he would find out sooner rather than later....he was right.

◆ ◆ ◆

Dom sought John out, and he found him in a quiet corridor. He was becoming impatient and needed to pick up the pace and get some answers before these *test subjects* arrived. He was a master of manipulation, in his own mind at least, and so should find out what he required.

John was a novice in this area; manipulation of any description did not sit comfortably with him.

"I hope that payment was to your liking?" Dom asked him.

John looked troubled. "I can't accept that much Mr Pearce."

"Please, it's a gift. You are, *perhaps,* retiring soon and it will come in useful."

"The thing is, do you want something in return?"

"A loyal employee is hard to find. You have done so much here. But, I'll tell you what, if you would like to give me something in return let me ask just two or three questions...curiosity has gotten the better of me. I know you would rather keep this whole subject secret, you aren't the type to blow your own trumpet, I can see that. It's to your credit. You don't even have to answer, if you feel bad about that, but if you don't *deny* what I ask you, I will take it as a *yes*, agreed? Then afterwards, I will drop the whole subject." He smiled. Dom had become obsessed with this power he'd seen; if he threw enough money at it he would get it, that's how it always worked out. John said nothing but looked at the lapels of Dom's white jacket, it did not feel wrong *not* to answer the questions, *or did it?* Dom continued. "Ok, first question; is it true you can *no longer* heal people?" John said nothing in response, "By the look on your face, I'll take that as a yes then,*...you* *can't any longer*. Second question, have you passed this gift that you had on to someone else, somehow? The new chef, Andy, for example?" Once again, unwittingly, John's face and the lack of a denial gave away the affirmative answer, "By the way, where is he?" Dom asked.

"I can't answer that."

"Sure you can. Given your recent, shall we say, motivation. Can't you tell me a little more? Or do you need more motivation?"

John felt a little violated by the assumption that his lack of answers might be based on money and not principal. Dom had a habit of eliciting that response; it came naturally to him.

"No, I don't want more money; I didn't really want the first lot."

"Keep it; it's already in your account. It's not like I don't have enough money. Ok then, one last question. Can this power to heal be passed on to… well...whom ever?" This was the key question to Dom. John did not know how to lie effectively, so again he gave the answer away by saying nothing, the look on his face, once again, said all that Dom required, "Thank you." said Dom, with all the information he needed, "Look, you have done nothing wrong my friend, enjoy retirement, and get a nice big boat." He placed his hand on John's shoulder. John did not remember telling Dom about his interest in getting a boat; *did he have this place bugged?* It was too late to reverse and deny anything; he hadn't actually *told* Dom anything anyway, not in actual words. He went back to his duties feeling the same uneasiness that he'd had before the conversation with Dom. He hoped that Andy was faring well at his end.

Dom immediately made a bee line for the kitchen; he strode in there to find Eric working away, preparing for the lunchtime service. Eric was surprised to see Dom, who rarely, if ever, made it into the kitchen.

"Eric, how are you?"

"Dominic! Fine, how are you?"

"Very well my friend."

"To what do I owe this honour?" Eric asked, semi sarcastically; he was one of the few members of the Haven's staff that didn't suck up to Dom. He didn't need this job either.

"Can't I call in and see my hard working staff from time to time?" Dom said, smiling, "You are staying on here I believe, part time; that's good to hear. Where is the new guy?"

"Andy? He's on leave, needed a couple of days off, so I'm covering for him."

"Oh I see, I just realised I haven't been in to welcome him yet. Is he settled in ok? When will he be back?"

"I don't know, but I'm fine until he gets back; he's flying back tomorrow, I believe."

Dom thanked Eric, told him it had been good to see him, and then he left. *That's it,* he thought, *this chef just needs to name his price and the power will be mine, he can pass it on to me. I'll have it.* Dom stuck his head back in the kitchen.

"Flying back from where exactly?"

"India."

"India? What's he been doing in India?"

"You'd have to ask him." Eric shrugged.

◆ ◆ ◆

Dom did some digging and he found out that Andy had jetted off to India for only two days. *Two days. What could he have possibly been doing in India for only two days; the travel alone was over sixteen hours.* It *must* have been something to do with the healing power, he thought. Of course he was right, but he didn't know any of the details. He would put his *proposition* to Andy at the first available opputunity. *I'll give you a lot of money to pass the gift on to me.* The Haven had become in grave danger of becoming a laughing stock if the healings were to stop, especially after the unfavourable news report. That also meant his own personal credibility would be damaged. *When* he was in possession of the power, he could call the shots. What he had created so far had served his ego well, but underneath, he himself knew just how fragile that ego was...like a tower of playing cards, waiting for someone to pull the one at the bottom.

*Everyone had a price,* that was one of the few valuable lessons his father had taught him, and he would find out what Andy's price was soon enough.

*The actual power to heal,* it made him smirk that it existed. Not the farcical shenanigans of the rituals that he performed or the performing priests in America, or the dubious *John of God. Actual supernatural healing power.* A less self absorbed person might have wondered at this phenomenon a little longer. Dom didn't, he just saw it as a tool he could use.

His plan was already formed; once he had gotten the power from Andy, he would cure someone with a high profile. That was his ticket to being a global superstar. No more messing around building up a slow following from relative obscurity. The sales of his machines and the backing of the WMA may have depended on these upcoming trials, but the sales and their backing paled into insignificance in comparison to what he could soon possess. He wouldn't even need them. It was now all so close that he could almost *touch* it.

# 35

In the hospital room, Jane held her daughters hand. The machines monitoring her were making the same sounds and displaying the same things as they did yesterday. *Did that mean she hadn't got any worse?* The induced coma the doctors had placed her in seemed to have slowed down her deterioration, or so they told her, but by how much it was impossible to say. The steady beeping of the monitor brought little comfort to Jane.

She'd had plenty of time to do some soul searching. Had she been wrong to want to move Fran and Jack far away from their father? What had motivated her to want to do so? Was it revenge on Andy for some reason, or was she simply flattered by the attention of someone else? She hadn't really known Rick all that well and she was going to uproot and move away from everyone she knew for him. It was madness really.

*Where was Andy?* The anger she had felt towards him in the last few months had evaporated and now he was simply the father of her children. He was on his way, so he'd said, and she felt that his presence here would make things better. She knew that he was the only other person on the planet that loved the children as much as she did.

◆ ◆ ◆

Andy's taxi turned on to familiar streets; he would be home soon. He intended to quickly pick up some cash, pay for the taxi, and then drive himself to the hospital as soon as possible, just in case he *could* heal Fran and had not already used up his daily chance. As the taxi pulled up outside his flat, he noticed a large 4x4 vehicle parked outside on the street, which was slightly unusual as such expensive cars were rarely seen in this neighbourhood. Still, he thought little of it, asked the taxi driver to wait and then ran inside to get some money from his sock drawer. As he did so, he saw a picture of Fran on the dresser; a seconds pause and he was on his way out again, hoping to God, once more, that he wasn't too late. It was now10:07 pm, dawn was at 6:10 am, he may have been *healing impotent* until then. He needed some more of that luck that had appeared to have changed for the better.

As he closed his front door, he noticed that two of the occupants from the 4x4 had gotten out and seemed to be standing, waiting for him, *or was that just his imagination?* They *were* looking in his direction at the very least. Andy paid the taxi fare and then turned around...the two men were closer. Andy recognised them from somewhere, but he couldn't quite place where.

"Andrew, could we have a word?" Gary, the taller of the two asked, "It is Andrew right?"

"Who are you?" Andy asked in return.

"Could we have a word...just a quick word?"

"About what?"

"It won't take a moment."

"I'm in a rush sorry." The second of the two heavys was Sean, he moved closer. He was twice the size of Andy and he gripped his arm, "What is this?"

"Don't worry, really." Gary said and then he grabbed him from the other side, "It's just a quick word." Andy tried to shrug them off, but soon realized that he couldn't do that very easily; especially in his current weakened state. They escorted him into the back of the 4x4. The two of them were not being *too* heavy handed and Andy hadn't pushed back too hard, not yet at least. It may have been a bit futile to fight these two gorillas, and he was curious to find out just what this was all about. He didn't have to wait for long. The front passenger seat's black tinted electric window whirred down to reveal Dom's smiling face.

"Hello Andrew." Dom said.

"Dominic?" Andy was surprised. Then he recognised where he had seen the two henchmen before: Sean and Gary were there on the interview day on the car park.

"Firstly, let me apologise for not coming to see you at the Haven. That was impolite of me. But, I wish to talk to you about something."

"If you wanted to talk, why didn't you just wait till I was back at work? What is all this about?"

"You seem to be a little too…unpredictable. India, where next I wonder? No, I needed to speak with you as soon as possible before you jetted off to God knows where else. By the way, why did you go to India?" Andy did not answer, but wondered how Dom had found out where he had been. The car set off slowly.

"Where exactly are we going? There is something that I need to take care of." Andy said.

"Not far." Dom replied.

"You can't just take me somewhere against my will, this is kidnapping."

"Kidnap, oh no, don't use that term. We are helping you. You see, we found out that you were, shall we say, *unstable,* it was particularly obvious with me being a qualified psychologist. Going off on wild goose chases, at goodness knows what expense. India, no less. For what reason? What would you tell the Police or anyone else for that matter, was your reason for going to India for two days when you had family problems? Your estranged wife's partner killed in a road accident just a few days previously....you were at the crash scene, correct? Your daughter seriously ill in hospital. It all sounds a bit odd, don't you think?"

"Where are you taking me? My phone will have a record of where we are going."

"My friend here has your phone and, conveniently, has switched it off and placed it in a lead box. This, believe it or not, is not the first time we have done this sort of thing." Andy checked his pocket and sure enough, his phone was missing, "There will be no record of this trip other than your memory." The car made a few turns; before long they passed over a canal bridge into a built up but disused industrial area, "All I want to do is talk for a while, nothing more."

"Then why bring me here?"

"More privacy." The car eventually stopped next to an old red brick building in the middle of the disused area. It looked like a former mill. There were no other cars or other people around. Andy was ushered out of the back of the car and into the building. Dom led the way as Andy was *guided* up several flights of stairs, before being pushed into a large empty room with banks of windows on either side. "All those steps, we really need to get a lift installed." Dom said. He waved his hands in the air, "What better place than this?

This room and one's just like it transformed the North West, not to mention Great Britain, into a global superpower. You can almost hear the rattle of the looms. Talking of *superpowers*." Dom gestured towards Andy with a smile.

Sean and Gary were stationed at the door, they had limited brain power between them and just followed instructions, asked no questions and were paid handsomely. They cared little for Dom; he was just another boss and they'd had better and worse gigs. Dom didn't need them often, but when he did, he paid them both well enough to more than sustain their cocaine habits which they had both continued since their time as drug-gang enforcers. They had formed a double act in prison, although both of them were playing the straight man role. Sean was serving time for armed robbery and Gary for GBH. Sean was the brains behind the two of them, if you could call it that; Gary was purely the muscle; even if he did like to do most of the talking. Dom asked them both to stand by the solitary door in the room, just out of their earshot. Andy asked.

"So what do you want from me?"

"Oh please, let's be frank, can't we? I know what you have." Dom said.

"Really, what's that?"

"Why *did* you go to India?"

"How do you know where I went?"

"You would be surprised at the amount of

information money can buy. Look, forgive this little *excursion;* I want you to be able to focus. Please don't tell me you went to India to pass on the power to someone else?"

Andy looked at Dom, but did not answer. For sure, this gift had been more trouble than it'd been worth and he would pass it on as soon as he could, but not quite yet.

"Is this your building?" Andy asked, trying to buy a bit of time to think.

"Yes, the whole area actually. There's nothing around here except old mills and canals. Until we transform it."

"Am I free to leave or am I not?"

"I have brought you somewhere quiet so that you can think clearly and make the *right decision.*"

"So I *can* go then?"

"Not just yet." Dom's face lost the smile and became more serious, "Just in case you hadn't already guessed, I want you to pass the power on to me. I believe you can do that."

"What if I don't have it, this power?"

"I think you do; I've seen the footage from the Haven. John has already said that he passed it on to you." Dom said, flatly. Andy looked surprised that John would tell him that. Perhaps Dom was lying. The strange thing was, 24 hours ago he didn't have it....he didn't even want it right now, but he couldn't give it up until he'd seen Fran. If he passed on the gift to Dom, using the method that John had instructed, he couldn't trust Dom to heal Fran first, or anything else for that matter; the *only* thing that mattered to Andy was saving Fran.

"I need time to think about it." Andy said.

"Why? I will make you rich. What's there to think about?"

"I want 24 hours before I make a decision" Andy said. *24 hours was not too long, but what if this chef decided to go missing again and this time not come back.* The power was way too close for him to risk him losing this gilt-edged opportunity to possess it.

"Very well, think it over." Dom beckoned to Sean, who opened the door, "We'll be back in the morning. I can't risk you doing a runner again, so make yourself comfortable. This should give you enough time to *think it over.*" He tossed Andy a bottle of water, "Don't bother shouting for help, there's no one around here." With that parting comment, he locked the door behind him and the three headed back to the 4x4. Dom was not going to let this chance of a lifetime pass him by. He meant business. Andy would probably be so shaken up by this that he wouldn't put up much resistance in the morning.

All Andy could see was the glow of the full moon as it cast shadows that came and went as the clouds passed in front of it. As Dom had said, there was no noise, nothing nearby, just the ticking of his wristwatch as time moved slowly towards dawn.

Back in the 4x4, Gary said, "Of course, we could lean on him, I mean *really* lean on him if he doesn't do what you want. Whatever that may be."

Dom stared straight ahead. He had already considered this option and worse. "We will see what tomorrow brings. If I get the feeling he is going to cause more problems, then we have other options. A night in there on his own should be enough to persuade him. There is no record of him being with us, the plates on this car are not traceable. But we can't just kill him off." Sean and Gary had taken out people before, in their drug war days, they had no issues about doing it again if needed; it just meant more money for them. The 4x4 eventually pulled up in another disused building, the number plates were changed and then Dom went his own way. *This fish was not going to leave the barrel.*

# 36

Jane had briefly closed her eyes. She thought she had cared deeply about Rick, but now that someone she *really* loved was at death's door, she realised that she hadn't. That didn't mean to say that she still loved Andy. *Had she ever?* Reality had hit hard; there was no longer a spark with Andy, but she now felt it was wrong to have treated him as she had done...he hadn't deserved that. Like it or not, she had taken the guilt at her own behaviour out on him. *But where the hell was he?* Him not taking things seriously had been one of her turn-offs, but right now, it wasn't about who had done this or hadn't done that, or who was in the ascendency, it was just about Fran, everything else had been stripped away.

She got up and paced around the hospital room for a time, her legs taking a minute to get full feeling back because she had been sitting down for so long. Then she sat back and watched Fran, looking tiny and frail amidst the multitude of machines, and hoped for a miracle.

◆ ◆ ◆

Andy sat against the wall near a window. It was getting cold in the long room. Shadows flickered and danced around the expanse of the mill floor, where at one time  in the not too distant past, dozens of looms would soon be clanking into action. Echoes of the racket they used to make seemed to reverberate around the now ghostly silent space. He got to his feet, feeling an overwhelming sense of panic. His watch said 2:08 am. An acute feeling of inertia hit him… he could not afford to wait till morning. Dom had seemed obsessed, like a prospector who had gone crazy in the pursuit of gold. He certainly could not be trusted.

Andy paced up and down in front of the window in search of inspiration, but in the room there was nothing that appeared useful to him, nothing that could put a dent in the heavy door blocking his exit. There was a length of rope, only about a meter long, with a metal stopper on one end and a couple of old filing cabinets. *Could he use the rope as a weapon perhaps?* He swung it back and forth. If he bashed the first one that came in through the door he might be able to get out, but that still meant waiting until tomorrow. He walked the whole length of the room. Being a former mill; it had large windows all down each side to let as much sunlight in as possible. On the other side of the room he could see a little more clearly what was below. It looked like he was about four stories up, maybe five. There was a small window ledge on the outside, about six inches deep going across the whole floor, though it was hard to see just how wide in the dark and from the inside.

His growing sense of impending doom and helplessness started to engulf him, it was almost out of control; he had to do *something*. He pulled one of the filing cabinets over to the window and with a big effort, pushed it over into a pane of glass, which smashed, sending glass flying and leaving rain bouncing in from outside. There were fragments of glass still in the window frame which Andy kicked at and eventually he had a space that looked big enough to get his body through. Sticking his head through first, he saw that the ledge was wide enough to fit his feet on, but only just. He was at least four floors up, not at the very top of the building, but high enough to kick start his fear of heights. Visibility was alright one moment but almost non-existent the next as the clouds periodically obscured the moons light. The rain was not heavy, but consistent. He waited for a break in the clouds and then as carefully as possible, he clambered out on to the ledge holding on to what he could for dear life, and not just his own. There was a drainpipe leading down to ground level further along, the kind he used to shimmy up and down as a kid; that was what he needed to get to. He was slightly shaking with fright, but the fear of something bad happening to Fran was over-riding his in-built desire for self preservation. The rain was dripping of his hair and nose as he clung on to the side of the building and he moved, one foot at a time, towards the drainpipe that was about twelve feet away. He made the error of looking down briefly and froze for a few seconds. He re-focused. After several more careful movements, he was halfway there, sliding his feet along the ledge rather than lifting them. The rain had made the ledge a little more slippery and many a year's build-up of algae wasn't helping, but before long, he *was* at the drain pipe. *What had he used to do as a kid?* Somehow it came back to him instinctively, as though he had done it just the day before; clasping both hands behind the pipe and supporting his weight with his feet at around a 45 degree angle to the wall, he moved one hand down at a time, getting a little lower each time. Progress was slow and steady, but he was doing it. Then, at around the third floor, there was a creaking noise as old bolts suddenly snapped and the drainpipe came away from the wall, leaving Andy in thin air. Gravity inevitably took over and he fell awkwardly to the ground below.

◆ ◆ ◆

Dom was at home, sitting at his desk, contemplating his options. If Andy was willing to take the cheque, then all well and good. If he resisted or refused, then plan 'b' would be put into action. He would be *forced* into doing it. The third possible option that he had thought about, the one where he offered Andy a job at the Haven as a healer, was completely off the table. He had rapidly gone off that idea because he now wanted the power exclusively for himself. The lure of the money from the machine sales was on the back burner, it was the power he wanted and now he had an unmissable chance to get his hands on it. *What can you give the person who has everything? More power and power corrupts as the saying goes.* Felicity brought him a drink.

"Busy day at work?" she asked.

"Quite." Dom replied.

"A penny for your thoughts?"

"They would only bore you." Dom smiled.

"You seem so wrapped up in your work, even more so lately." she said, "You are doing so much good, I am so proud of you."

"I get the feeling things are going to get even better soon." Dom said, with a wry smile.

"Why's that sweet?"

"Just a feeling a corner is going to be turned

soon... with the healing."

"You're so selfless." she said, with a kiss to his forehead.

"I was lucky to be born into money, it would be wrong not to help those less fortunate."

"Shame the whole worlds not like you; it would be a better place."

Dom smiled again, kissed his wife on the forehead, then wondered about the best way to kill Andy and then dispose of the body, if necessary of course.

◆ ◆ ◆

The rain wasn't letting up. Andy lay flat out on his back, the long drop having been broken only by the hard ground. He opened his eyes slowly and saw the moon and the droplets of rain coming towards him. *How long had he been unconscious?* He was awake and reality, however strange as it was, came back to him in rapid stages. He remembered falling and then what he had to do; what he didn't know yet was whether or not he could move after the fall. He was resistant to try, just in case he couldn't. He went for it, his left leg then right leg then both arms. *Nothing broken*, it seemed, and slowly he got to his feet. He looked up at where the drainpipe had broken and it seemed quite high up, yet he had come out relatively unscathed; was that the *never get ill bonus?* It was not the time to wonder, it was time to move and instinctively he set off in one direction; eventually he would come across something that would give him his bearings and from there he could find his way to the hospital. His wristwatch had been broken in the fall, but the sky was still black...dawn was not here yet. He moved at a steady pace through the landscape until he came across the old canal, used to transport the cotton and cloth from yester-year, now used by barges for leisure trips. He figured that if he followed the canal it would end up *somewhere* and he would not end up going around in circles. He moved onwards and eventually, he came to a crossroads that he remembered from the journey in the 4x4. *He was going the right way.* Jogging with a slow but steady pace he eventually reached more built-up areas and he could see the lights of the football stadium off in the distance. He knew, roughly, where the hospital was from there and so he just kept moving, periodically looking upwards to see if dawn was any closer.

# 37

Dom had woken from a dream. He didn't often wake up in the middle of the night, but tonight the feeling from the dream had been so strong it was as though it had jolted him back into consciousness. The dream was set way back in the past. It was sunny, and he was walking in front of the sea, thousands of adoring people wearing simple clothing followed him and hung on to his every syllable. *Power and recognition. A status of almost biblical proportions.*

He went downstairs as his wife lay sleeping. The rain was beating against the French doors as he unlocked the safe that was hidden behind the picture of the Haven in the study. He grabbed bundles of notes, some twenties, some fifties, counted out £100,000 worth and then placed them in a sports bag, before covering them over with a towel. He wanted no record of a bank transfer this time, doing that with John may have been a big mistake. There were to be zero links back to him; not now that the stakes had been raised.

This was the easiest option for him: people *always* listened to money. This chef, Andy, looked like he'd never had any real money, nor would he *ever* have any. This was going to be a good opportunity for him to get out of relative poverty. If he wouldn't accept the money or looked like causing a problem, then there was always plan "b", or *how to force someone into doing something they don't want to*. Dom didn't exactly see himself as one of the Kray twins, but he would use whatever tactics that were necessary. *Nothing* was going to stop him with this. Dom placed the sports bag down on the kitchen floor. He saw his reflection in the mirror, smiled, then went upstairs and climbed back under the covers.

◆ ◆ ◆

Andy kept moving, though he was now rain-soaked completely wet and looked like he had fallen into the canal. He tried to flag down a passing taxi, but the driver took one look at him, mouthed "sorry" and drove on. He was getting nearer...slowly, but every muscle in his body was being *forced* to move, the extra weight of his wet clothes making it even more difficult for him to keep up a decent pace. If he'd had his phone on him he could have called Jane or the hospital or John. All he could do was keep moving towards what was still well over a mile away.

A police patrol car pulled over alongside him.

"You alright sir?" Officer Jenkins in the passenger seat asked him. He was a similar age to Andy.

"Look, I need to get to the hospital. Can you take me? Please." Andy said, though he was quite breathless.

"Have you been drinking? You are a little wet."

"No, no I haven't. My daughter is in hospital, I need to get there as soon as possible."

"Where have you been tonight sir?"

"I don't have time to explain, I just need to get there." The two officers looked at each other; they didn't really want a soaking wet passenger in the back of their patrol car.

"I think that you need to go home and dry off." Jenkins said.

"I intend to, but I need to get to the hospital first." Jenkins was not convinced that Andy had *not* been drinking; by the way he was both struggling to speak and was swaying. Many drunks said that they needed to get to the hospital when asked where they were going, it was their go-to response, or so it seemed. Jenkins decided that this drunk didn't look too problematic though. He had no grounds or desire to take him in to the station.

"Get yourself home and dry off sir. Sleep it off." The patrol car set off again, "At least the rain will sober him up a bit." he said to the driver and they resumed their patrol.

Andy continued walking forwards; then all at once he felt a pain from the back of his head, adrenaline had numbed it for the past several minutes, but it must have been from when he hit the ground. His hand tentatively felt the back of his head and, sure enough, there was a lump that was sore to the touch, he felt a pulse of nausea go through his whole body. He took a few more steps and then dropped down to his knees. Supporting himself with both his hands on the ground, he went lower and lower until his face was on the tarmac.

◆ ◆ ◆

Officer Jenkins finished making the sandwiches at the police station, and he took a tray of them, along with cups of tea, to the overnight stays in the cells that they had for the trouble-makers and the drunks. Quiet night: only two of the cells were occupied. He opened the first cell door and passed a tea and a sandwich to the eighteen year old who hadn't been able to handle his drink the previous night. In the second cell, he passed the tea to Andy who had been awoken by Jenkins's footsteps.

"Sore head?" Jenkins asked.

"Where am I? Did you arrest me?" Andy asked.

He'd been flat out for a while.

"Drunk tank; if you wanna call it that. You just needed to sleep it off. Face down in the street is hardly the best way to spend the night."

"What time is it?"

"12:30."

"Am? Night time?"

"You *did* drink a lot. We dried you off by the way." Jenkins said. Andy looked at his clothes: they were a basic grey coloured sweatshirt and pants. "12:30 lunchtime."

"Shit, I need to make a call."

"Wife wondering where you are?"

"Sort of."

"We would have let her know, but you had no ID on you; not even a phone. Come through to the desk, let's take some details, you looked in a bad way when we found you face down in the rain. At least you weren't sick." Andy did feel physically sick, as he gave his name, date of birth and address. He called Jane's number from the station, luckily he had it memorized. He waited for an answer; it connected and then there was silence.

"Jane? Jane?" He could hear her breathing so he knew she was on the other end, "How is Fran? Jane please, how is Fran?" There was no answer for what seemed like an eternity, and then Jane did find some words.

"You are too late." Then she ended the call.

"Jane, Jane?!" Andy called back, but she did not

answer a second time.

"Sounds like you are in trouble; she'll come around in a day or two. Get her some flowers." Jenkins said. It wasn't strictly police proceedure to make chit-chat like that, but Jenkins could tell that Andy was a decent guy, like himself. Andy was numb; he didn't react to Jenkins, he just stared into space. Eventually, he asked if he could leave, Jenkins said that he could and also to return the borrowed clothes within a day or two. He gave him a black bin bag to take his wet clothes in; Andy had no interest in them. "Pick them up later if you want." Jenkins said. Still Andy did not talk. In a trance he put his shoes on, "Are you sure you are ok?" Jenkins asked. Andy forced a nod and then left the police station. Sure enough, outside it was daylight, the sun was actually out. He started placing one foot in front of the other, but walking aimlessly in a random direction. *You're too late* reverberated around in his head.

◆ ◆ ◆

Dom unlocked the door with the excitment level of a kid opening his presents at christmas. Everything that he wanted, for now, was in this room. The prize was almost his. He pushed the door open and strode in, closely followed by Sean and Gary. A blast of cold air hit his face. *Where was he hiding?* "He's gone." Gary had a knack for stating the obvious.

◆ ◆ ◆

Their black 4x4 had been driving around in circles since just after 8:00 am. Dom and his two henchmen had unlocked the old mill door to find Andy gone and a gust of wind blowing through the smashed glass window. They had worked out his escape route easily, but were not sure where he was now. They knew, judging from his footprints in the mud, which direction he had set off in, but the trail had soon been lost. He was somewhere out there, but they had no way of knowing *when* he had made his great escape and how far it was that he had got. They had already been to the Haven and also to his flat, but there was no sign of him anywhere. Right now Dom's biggest fear was that he might have disappeared again...for good. He'd felt relieved that jumping out of the window hadn't killed him: he was of no use to him dead... not until he'd passed on the power.

Then, after turning another corner, Gary in the passenger seat saw Andy sitting on a bench, just staring at the ground and taking in heavy breaths.

"That's him isn't?" he said to Dom, who was in the back of the car, "He's changed his clothes, but that's him."

"Pullover." Dom instructed Sean to stop

alongside the bench. Andy saw the car and it registered whose it was, but nothing would snap him out of the trance-like state he was in. He didn't move an inch. Dom spoke from the car; he wasn't sure if there was any public CCTV in this area and did not want any recordings of this episode. "Andrew? Or is it Steve McQueen? Look I am sorry it came to this, I only wanted you to have time to think, uninterrupted. On reflection, it probably wasn't the best idea I've have ever had." Andy looked up slowly to see Dom's smiling face. It was all *his* fault, if he hadn't derailed his journey, Andy might have been in time to save Fran. *You are too late.* Something broke through the trance he was in….*rage* and *hate*. "Why don't you come with us? I have something for you." Andy looked at the expression-less face of Gary in the front seat, then back at Dom's false smile. He stood up; this time he needed no coercing. Slowly he walked to the back of the 4x4, Dom slid over and Andy got in. Still he had said nothing; it was almost as if he couldn't speak. They were in their own bubble, in the back of the 4x4 with blacked out windows; Dom might as well get the deal done then and there, rather than risk something else happening. He had the fish on the hook; this time it wasn't going to wriggle free. Andy still just looked straight ahead. "Have you had time to decide? I hope this might help you make your decision." He zipped open the bag and removed the towel to reveal the bundles of notes, "One..hundred..thousand." Dom said slowly, "Plus, you know that I will use the power for good. It's a win-win." Andy slowly turned to face Dom; he waited a while and then gave a single nod, "Excellent." Dom said with a straight face, "I knew you would do the right thing. Get yourself a nice Range Rover." he joked. Andy looked ahead again. Dom put a more serious face on, "What do you need to do, to pass it on to me?"

Andy finally spoke. "It's quite simple. We need somewhere quiet where I can concentrate." he said, quietly.

"Where do you want to go?" Dom asked.

"The Haven might be fitting."

"Yes, you're right. You are *so* right." Dom instructed Sean to head for the Haven, "I'll call ahead; I want to make an announcement. I'll get someone to film it for the news and youtube and whatever." Dom called Penny and asked her to rapidly set up a gathering. He looked at his watch. "How long does it take to swap it over to me?" he asked Andy.

"Not long." Andy replied. Dom planned the mini gathering for two hours time, set up in the majestic grounds of the Haven, with all of the staff and whoever else was concerned present. He called the newspapers to ask them to send a reporter to this *significant, unmissable* event. He considered calling Leach, but thought it better *he* found out *after* the WMA had green lit the financial backing. That amused him. *Not long now*, before he could make the world aware of his gift to humanity.

◆ ◆ ◆

Eric was standing at the back door of the kitchen having a smoke; quite happy to be plodding along working several days in a row. It's that old thing, if you don't *have* to do something, then you don't mind doing it as much. Truth be told, he was now enjoying working here at the Haven as much as he ever had anywhere. He felt rejuvenated and enthusiastic. He noticed Dom's white Range Rover stir up dust on the gravel path that led to the Haven. It usually cruised along at a slow pace, but today it was travelling with more gusto. Sean was driving and he had two passengers, one of which was Dom, the other... well it looked like Andy. Eric thought that a little odd, as Dom rarely engaged with the *lower ranking* members of staff and he had never even been in to see Andy since he had started. The Range Rover drove around and parked up at the back, out of sight. The three occupants got out and went in the back entrance. Andy noticed that there was no sign of John's car on the car park and once inside, there was no whirring of the buffer machine to be heard either.

"Let's go to the healing room." Dom suggested. Andy nodded. All three headed down to the basement and Dom pulled out a set of keys to unlock the healing room door. Once inside, he flicked a switch to illuminate the room. "No need for the candles." he said. Then he instructed Sean to wait outside the door; so that Andy could not change his mind and make a run for it, "Ok. So, do what you have to do." Andy was still in a dream-like state, still not in much of a state to do anything. He looked closely at Dom. Inside he was feeling complete disgust and hatred, stronger than he had felt for Rick. He held Dom responsible for him being too late to get to Fran. It didn't matter about anything else or who else might share part of the blame, at this moment Andy was holding Dom *fully* responsible. He knew that he had to be there for Jack's sake, so his urge to pick up one of the ornate candle sticks and batter Dom over the head with it was resisted. He had a different idea.

"Hold out your hand." Andy said.

"Which one?" Dom asked.

"Doesn't matter." Dom held out his right hand. Andy looked right into Dom's eyes, so intently that it made Dom, who was usually emotionally untouchable, feel uncomfortable. Andy took his own right hand and grasped Dom's in a handshake. Still looking into his eyes, but now with a blank expression, Andy began to empty his mind and just clear it of everything. Then he began to concentrate, he thought of everyone that he had healed since he got the gift, but in a way he hadn't done before. He focused on everything at once, whilst still remaining blank on the outside. Then his eyes closed. This went on for a minute or so; Dom was beginning to become restless and more than a little puzzled. Then Andy placed his left hand on top of Dom's, as John had done with him weeks earlier. Dom felt a shock of something, it was like a jolt of electricity going through his entire body. He was left with a tingling sensation. Andy released his grip and his hands fell once again to his sides.

"Is that it? Is it done?" Dom asked.

"It is done." Andy replied.

"As simple as that. I do feel different, it's amazing." Dom looked at himself in the mirror and smiled even more broadly. *The power to heal,* he whispered to himself. He stared at himself a little longer, before spinning back around. "You did the right thing." he said to Andy, "Here." He passed him the bag of money, "Of course you still have your job, if you want it. But this little event is strictly between us, agreed?" Andy nodded in agreement. There was a knock at the door and Sean stuck his head in the room.

"The press guys are here." he said.

"I'm on my way." Dom said. He tapped Andy on the shoulder and then passed him his phone back; he no longer had any need to communicate with this chef. Then he strolled off through the ornate door and into the corridor.

In the grounds of the Haven, Penny had set up a podium with a number of chairs in front. The sun was shining and everyone that Dom wanted there had arrived. The news reporters were ready and most of the staff were present to hear this big announcement from Dom. *What was it going to be? Had they gotten the big contract?* Dom did like to blow his own trumpet, he wasn't exactly low key, but it was the first time he had ever done something like this. Eric had also left the kitchen and come out into the grounds; Andy saw him and walked over to him.

"Are you ok? When did you get back?" Eric asked.

"Not great Eric. I can't explain right now. I'm probably not coming back." Andy replied.

"Oh. That is not good to hear. Dominic came in looking for you for some reason, when you were in India." Eric noticed how down and dishevelled Andy looked: unshaven and still in the basic grey clothes from the police station, "If I can help in any way, let me know." They stopped talking and saw that Dom had come out of the gleaming white building and was making his way over to the portable lectern in preparation for his big announcement. The banner and logo for the WMA consortium had been placed next to the plinth. Dom had no microphone to address his audience, but then neither had Jesus.

# 38

Ramesh put down the book that he was reading when he heard a gentle knock at the door. He got up out of his favorite chair and opened the door to see a young woman standing there. In her arms she held her six month old son. Ramesh smiled at the woman and then the child. He placed his hand upon the small frame of the coughing youngster . Soon afterwards, his coughing stopped and the young woman looked warmly at Ramesh, her eyes full of gratitude. This quite frail looking old man had healed her son. *Never leave India*. It was not every day that people came to him to be cured, but it was *most* days. The hospitals were here in Lucknow were not bad, but not quite good enough to accomodate everybody in need, and some things that he could do, they simply couldn't. Nor could anywhere else.

He took a walk out in to the small patch of garden that was his. A mild breeze was rustling the leaves of the Banyan tree, twelve feet away from his front door. It was quite rare to have such a tree growing in this vicinity and it was the only one in a twenty mile radius. It had started to grow here, just after Ramesh had made this house his home. He sat under it, on the ground. He liked to be physically near its roots. When he sat there in that place, he felt more connected and more in tune with *everything*.

He thought about Andy and his unfortunate predicament; but at least he knew that now he had some hope of saving his daughter. The future was always uncertain, even with Ramesh's insight and powers, but hope sprang eternal.

◆ ◆ ◆

Several hours earlier, John watched the rain drops hit and roll down the glass of his living room window which overlooked a small park. He liked to just sit there and watch people walk by; some walking their dogs, some jogging, some pushing prams. Often, when he'd had the healing gift, he could see an aura around them as they walked. Sometimes light, some neutral, some people with no discernable aura and occasionally, some with darkness. This had been a part of the gift: to be able to sense the vibrations and essence that everyone unknowingly emits. John had sensed Dom's vibration to be particularly low, which made him feel like an empty vessel. That was one of the reasons why he'd always felt slightly uncomfortable when interacting with him. Having said that, he wasn't the only one, there were plenty of people like him walking around. Quite a shocking percentage. He had realised that sobering fact quite soon after getting the gift. When he, in turn, had passed the gift on to Andy, the ability to see and read auras had gone with it. Today then, he was wondering why he saw a faint glow above someone walking across the park. A similar thing had happened the previous day, although he had dismissed that as probably just light reflecting off something. *This second occasion lessoned the probability. Was there a rainbow somewhere, refracting light above this person walking along?* There didn't appear to be a rainbow anywhere; just a grey mist. *Slightly Odd,* he thought, although nothing about life ever seemed *that* odd ever since the day that he had inherited the gift. The other thing was, he could read people a little better, or so he thought. It didn't feel like it did before, not quite, but something like it. In the few weeks he'd gone without the gift he had almost gotten used to being just o*rdinary John.* He decided to call Peter; perhaps he might be lucky again and catch him on one of his better days.

When the call came, Peter was indulging in his favourite pastime of watching old black and white films. Today it was *The thing from another world.* He liked the old films more than new ones, especially science fiction and Marx Brothers comedies. Even with *some* Alzheimer's he could still recite a lot of the routines from the Marx Brothers. He said out loud to himself, *the remake is better, the only time ever that the remake is better.* His phone rang.

"Hello?" Peter answered.

"Peter, it's John."

"John, how are you doing?"

"I'm good thanks, how are you?" John asked, he could hear the noise of the tv the background. Peter was distracted by the film and the creature bursting through the door.

"Amazing special effects these, for the year 1951. Even if it is just a tall man in a suit."

"Is that a film you are watching?"

"Yes, one of the classics. Kurt Russell is good in the 1982 remake. John Carpenter, I believe."

"*The Thing*? Yes, yes he is. Peter, I want to ask you something."

"Thirty one years after the original. Thirty one! Go ahead."

"Peter, it's about the gift." John said. Peter paused the film.

"Go on."

"You know after you passed it on to me. Did you ever see aura's around people again or anything like that, weeks later?"

"Aura's or reading people you mean? Little lights?"

"Yes, or did it all just stop when you passed the gift on."

"It stopped on the very same day. Why, you been getting them signs?"

"I think so."

"That boy you passed the gift on to, you said he lost the gift and it got reversed. Touch of death?"

"That's right."

"Well, you can probably guess what's happened." Peter un-paused the film and the man in the monster suit continued on his rampage.

"What Peter?"

"He's lost it, so it's come back to you. The gift I mean." Peter said, flatly.

"Is that possible? He is on a mission right now to try and get it back."

"Possible? Anything is possible in this life; you should know that by now. Darn thing wasn't just gonna disappear into thin air." Peter said, matter-of-factly. This did actually make some sense to John: when the gift left Andy it returned to whence it came...himself. Like a spirit returning.

"Peter, you think the gift has returned to me, I think you might be right. Thank you Peter, I'll be in touch, take care." John ended the call and Peter turned the tv volume up again.

◆ ◆ ◆

There had been no word from Andy. John felt partly responsible, if not mainly responsible for what had happened to Andy's daughter. If the power to heal had returned to him like a boomerang, he knew that he must go to the hospital at once and hope that it was not too late. John thought about a plan, *how would he get in and get close enough to Fran?* He put on his cleaners uniform and headed out to his car. He took the route to the hospital he had travelled many times: he had previously worked there for five years. Before long he arrived and then solemnly parked up. He got out swiftly and entered the hospital's main doors. He knew where the children's critical ward was...that was where she would be. As he walked, he wondered if Andy had already got back from India with all the twists and turns, Andy had forgotten to let John know the current state of affairs; unless something had happened to him. When John had rung Andy, it had gone straight to voicemail.

It was actually classed as an offense to impersonate hospital staff, even the cleaners. You needed an ID to walk the corridors freely, though John drew little unwanted attention with his uniform on, which was more or less identical to the hospital standard one. He had put blue latex gloves on to avoid accidentally making skin contact with anyone else. He headed to Francesca's ward as quick ly as he could. When he arrived he saw two doctors in the corridor. They were talking quietly but John heard that they were discussing Francesca's condition. Signs of her brain activity were very low and her mother had been informed that the machine keeping her alive would eventually be switched off. Then they both headed off in different directions. She was still alive, but only by a hair's breadth it seemed. The door to the room was open and Jane was sitting in a chair; the only adult in the room. Fran was in the hospital bed, motionless, any remaining life force slowly ebbing out of her. John put a hospital mask on and then he walked in. He greeted Jane with a nod, she looked as drained as he'd ever seen anyone look. He went over to the bed. He picked up some empty cups and then, before doing anything else, placed his hand on Fran's hand. Jane was so exhausted she didn't pay much attention as to why the cleaner was doing that...he obviously meant no harm. He left his hand there for a few seconds, emptied his mind, and then concentrated on healing this small child. When he felt like the time was enough, he pulled his hand away. He smiled at Jane from beneath the mask. That was all he could do; if he *was* able to heal again, it would soon be discovered.

Exactly what was happening with this gift was not clear. It was all confusing and mixed up. Forces way beyond any rationality were at work here. All he could do now was let time pass and see what happened. He walked outside, slowly this time, got back into his car and waited it out.

# 39

At the Haven, Dom was almost ready to deliver his big announcement. Soon the conglomerate was going to invest in his growing company, and now that *he* had the gift there could be no longer any doubt about that. It was time to reveal to the world the power he possessed. Andy watched proceedings, along with the others, with a morbid curiosity. Eric also wanted to see what this clown was going to come up with next. Sue was stood with the other ladies from the office and all the staff were all hoping that, whatever this was, it might lead to a pay rise.

The camera was at the ready, the audience was ready and starting to fidget. Dom was almost ready, with Felicity at his side, almost *presidential* in stature...at least in *his* mind. He stood, poised, and then he began to talk.

"Today we stand on the verge of a significant breakthrough at the Haven. Our loyal staff members here have worked tirelessly and with great determination to help propel us into the position we are in today. In the next few days, a deal with the consortium, the WMA, will be finalised and we will enter the next phase in our growth. With their backing, next year we intend to open a sister facility in London and also one in Glasgow. But that will be just the beginning. Our future is bright and the future of the people that we can help looks brighter still." Dom said, sounding not unlike a politician. He paused and whispered to Penny. "Are the two patients the WMA sent ready to be brought out?" His assistant, Penny, gave the affirmation, "Bring them out." She left and with the help of another member of staff they brought out the two patients the WMA had sent to test the veracity of their investment. The patients had each undergone two days of treatments with the machines. Ryan Leach and the WMA awaited any improvements in their condition with eagerness and also a little trepidation. These patients, who may have or may not have been aware of their guinea pig status, had been vetted and chosen by themselves, and that meant there could be no manipulation of the truth here.

Now that Dom had the power, there was no need for him to worry about whether the machines worked or not. If, or rather when, he healed these two people, right here and now in front of this gathering, the deal with the WMA would become more and more irrelevant. Perhaps he wouldn't even sign it.

The first patient was wheeled out by Penny: he was a sixty seven year old man by the name of Christopher Smith. He had leukaemia. The WMA were not messing around or making it easy with these trials, they'd thrown Dom a curve ball straight off. If the Haven could cure Christopher, then they had something. Even if they prolonged his life, it would definitely have been something to look at. Christopher was quite frail looking in the chair; shivering slightly, even though he was covered in several blankets on a warm day. On his face were several small bruises. He coughed intermittently. He and his family were willing to try any potential cure and he had spent the last twenty four hours receiving intensive treatment on the machines, although there was no apparent change in his condition, yet.

Dom approached Christopher and gently placed his hand, just as he had seen John do on the CCTV, on his forehead. The gathered audience looked on and wondered what was going to happen next; they all knew that Dom held faith healing sessions, but never before in public. Nothing happened immediately; Penny wheeled Christopher a few feet away as the second patient was brought in: Winifred Hall, aged seventy one, had rheumatoid arthritis; her knee joints were so swollen and stiff that she couldn't really walk at all, her elbow joints were not much better.

Another curve ball, as the consortium saw it. This place was going to have to be good to get their money and if *was* that good it would be a no lose investment. Winifred had extensive treatment on the tables, specifically, electronic pulses through crystals to her joints. She had said that they felt a little less painful, or so she thought. Dom repeated the healing process, though this time he held the patients hand, as he had seen Andy do, for around ten seconds. *That should do it.* He had felt a strange sensation each time that he had made contact with the patients, something he'd never felt before, but neither pleasant nor unpleasant. How long it was going to take he didn't know exactly, but the time that he'd put in tracking John's and Andy's healing exploits, he knew that it wouldn't be too long. He checked to see if the man with the camera was still filming, then looked to address the ensemble once again.

"I know that most of you gathered here know about the faith healing that we practice here at the Haven. It's true that I have never gone too public about this, but, starting from today, I think it is time to really push the message of what we stand for. Man and machine working in perfect harmony. And, like I have said before; modern science and ancient methods coming together in a perfect union. Are there any questions?" he asked. Andy was still watching the proceedings with a blank expression. Part of him knew that he would have to pull himself together at some point soon for Jack's sake. As of right now, he was watching Dom as the shark that had just bitten your leg off. A news reporter prepared himself to ask a question.

"Are you saying it's a done deal with the consortium then Mr Pearce?"

"It's as good as done, yes. Not signed or sealed, but *almost* delivered." Dom replied. The reporter noticed the odd blemish on Dom's face.

"And will they be financing the expansion; the other facilities that you plan to open next year?"

"Not 100%, but the majority." Dom replied. Then he started to cough. He asked Penny to get him some water; she scurried off and came back with a bottle. Dom took a gulp and then started to speak again, "So what I was saying..." he started to cough again, this time more deeply. His face seemed to have more of a rash, than just a few blemishes. He took another drink, "Excuse me. Slight frog." he said, in between coughs. The water did not seem to be making much difference. He looked at his assistant for help; she looked back at him, puzzled. He dropped the bottle of water and then bent down to pick it up, except he couldn't....he couldn't bend down properly. His knees were so stiff, he couldn't move them and the pain was severe. Penny moved in quickly to get the water.

"Are you alright Dominic?" she asked quietly.

Dom looked across at the two patients in the wheelchairs; both of them suddenly looked healthier, then he looked down at the grass of the Haven's cultured lawn, he dropped to it with a searing headache to match the pain in his joints. All the while the camera kept filming. All the attention was on, not Dom, but the two patients who seemed to have made miraculous recoveries, their symptoms suddenly disappearing. Dom, meanwhile, was looking quite ill. The gathered audience was not sure what was going on, some thought it was perhaps some pre-prepared stunt to promote the Haven; some sort of show. Most of the focus was on Winifred and Christopher, who were now both slowly walking around, no one was really noticing Dom's distress. Except for Andy.

"What the hell is going on?" Eric asked Andy. Andy did not answer, but it looked like, to him only, that Dom had not just cured, but taken on himself the ailments of the two patients he had just laid his hands on. *Had he absorbed the illness rather than cure it?* Andy had not wished for that specifically when he passed the power on to Dom, but his intentions were not as Dom expected them to be, "Have you ever seen anything like that?" Eric continued, as Dom was helped into a chair himself. Winifred was standing on her own two feet, still a little tentatively, for the first time in five years. The majority of the watching crowd still thought this was some kind of publicity stunt. With regards to Dom, some of the observers thought that perhaps he himself had been feeling unwell earlier, which would explain him not looking so good right now.

"That's it, thank you, that is all for today." Penny said, politely and quickly, before she helped Dom back through the doors of the Haven. Feeling generally confused, the gathering dispersed, whispering and trying to figure out what they had just seen. One reporter felt like he had been tricked in some way and that his time had just been wasted. There was nothing concrete here he could use and it looked like the whole thing got cut short for some reason. He packed away his equipment, whilst muttering to himself and then he headed off, along with the others.

Inside the Haven, Dom instructed Penny to take him down to the faith healing room. Felicity looked worried, but did not have anything to offer in terms of help, she followed sheepishly.

"Do you not want to go to the treatment rooms?" Felicity asked him. He shook his head and, grabbing a piece of paper, he scribed *get me Andr* before having to stop.

"Andrew? *Chef* Andrew?" Penny asked, he was the only *Andrew* they knew. He nodded. "What for?" The look in his eyes persuaded her not to argue. Felicity looked on helplessly, she was no use to Dom right now; she never actually was more than just fuel to his ego. Any originality or individuality she'd had when they had first met had been systematically drained out of her. Penny left and made her way back to the Haven's grounds where she'd spotted Andy earlier. Hurriedly, she approached him.

"Dominic wants to speak with you, I don't know why, but I think it's urgent. There seems to be something wrong with him."

Andy paused for a moment, and then spoke in response. "Tell him.....tell him I quit." He turned to face Eric, "I'll be seeing you Eric. I'll get in touch sometime."

"You are going somewhere?" Eric asked.

"Yeah, don't know where, but not here. It was good to meet you." With that, Andy picked up the bag of money and started walking through the grounds to make his way to the hospital. He knew that Jack was going to need him more than ever now. As he passed the sign *Welcome to the Haven*, he wished that he had never seen or heard of the place. He kept walking until he saw a taxi at the side of the road. He was going to walk the whole several miles to the hospital, but realised he needed to get there as soon as possible. He thought about calling Jane again, but decided against it.

Before too long, the taxi arrived at the hospital. The driver normally made chit-chat with his passengers, but in this case he had not bothered to; he'd never seen a passenger look so *distant* in the twenty years he'd been driving a taxi cab. What had happened to Dom offered no respite from the huge burden...the black hole, that Andy had fallen into. He had to carry on, somehow.

# 40

An hour passed by, and then, in the rear view mirror of his car, John noticed a taxi pull up in the hospital car park with someone in the passenger seat who looked familiar: it looked like it was Andy. John had no idea what condition Fran was in and whether or not his efforts had been successful. He took a deep breath, got out of his car and followed Andy as he headed towards the reception. Andy asked where his daughter was and how she was. *You are too late*, was all that Jane had said to him. A member of staff on reception told him which ward she was on, and that he would need to ask the doctor on duty about her condition. He left reception and followed the instructions on how to get to the ward. Then he heard someone call his name from behind.

"Andy." John said quietly. Andy turned to see a cleaner who knew his name, then he realised who it was.

"John. What are you doing here?"

"I came to see if I could help. Did you get the

gift back?" John asked. Andy nodded once.

"Got it back, too late." Andy said and then he turned and continued on to Fran's ward. John followed him.

◆ ◆ ◆

The news about the two successful healings had reached Ryan Leach fairly quickly. They had set Dom and the Haven two difficult tasks in Christopher and Winifred; nigh on *impossible* tasks in Leach's opinion but, amazingly, they were both healed in just 48 hrs. The place really *did* have something. The figures he'd seen were legit. Leach had phoned Dom to tell him the good news; two out of four successes they had required... the Haven had achieved two out of two. The trial was done and dusted and the WMA consortium was ready to put its considerate financial backing into his project. The green light had been given and they wanted Dom signed up with them as quickly as they could. The only slightly worrying thing was, Dom was not answering his phone and was unavailable for comment. They had only a verbal agreement, a handshake: nothing had been signed by either party. *Perhaps Dom had re-considered*? Had the WMA been in the wrong to make him jump through some more hoops? After all, the figures had already looked impressive. Leach's superiors might blame him personally if the deal fell through, but then he had only *suggested* a final *fool-proof* test using four more patients of *their* choosing. They had agreed to it. It was good, logical, business sense. He would keep trying Dom's phone every hour or so.

◆ ◆ ◆

Dom was not thinking about his phone or the WMA or Leach. He was not in a good way. The doctor had been called, the *actual* doctor and he was en-route to the Haven. Penny was trying to comfort Dom as best she could and Felicity held his hand as he tried to get his breath.

"Were you ill this morning? You should have postponed this till later in the week." she said.

"No, I was fine. Where is Andrew?" Dom asked, in a croaky voice.

"He's not coming. I can't find him." Penny stated. She didn't say that he had quit. She did wonder why Dom wanted the *chef,* above anyone else. It all seemed very odd.

The Doctor duly arrived, but Dom already knew what had happened, he had been given the power to heal alright, but with the *slight* drawback of taking on the patient's illness himself. Not much use to him. Had Andy done this deliberately? Dom suspected that he had. Or had something gone wrong in the transferral process? He knew that these were strange and, most probably, unpredictable forces that they were playing around with.

The Doctor did some routine tests, but he could not find a solution or explanation as to Dom's sudden collapse and symptoms...which was understandable, as he only dealt in *by the textbook* medicine. Dom was dismissive and played down his new symptom's seriousness. He knew that the doctor had no answer to his problems. The doctor gave him some strong pain killers, told him to rest up, take vitamins and to see how he was over the next couple of days. He suggested that his symptoms might be down to stress from overwork, or a virus. It wouldn't look impressive, from the Haven's point of view, to have an actual *real* doctor on the premises, as they traded on *alternative* methods, so they showed him out of the side door.

Dom knew what he needed, and it wasn't rest or anti-biotics. He sent for Sean. Within half an hour, Sean arrived, not shocked at all, it seemed, to see Dom in the faith healing room, in a wheelchair and covered in blankets. He'd half-heard the mutterings and whispered conversations recently and had gathered that there was something *unusual* taking place. Gary had no idea, but then he wasn't the *brains* of the duo. Not much could surprise or concern Sean and as long as he was getting paid well, that was all that mattered. If he had been asked to help find the *Holy Grail*, he would have said "*fine, how much are you paying me*?" Dom cleared the room of everyone except Sean.

"Get me Andrew. Find that son of a bitch and bring him here. I don't care how you do it." Dom said, in a raspy voice, "You know where he lives. Check the hospital, I hear his daughter is in there." Sean didn't say anything, he just nodded, then left. Dom looked around at the set up that had given false hope for so many people that he had performed his faith healing *act* on. This chef was going to pay for double-crossing him, but first, he was going to fix whatever it was that he had done.

◆ ◆ ◆

Andy reached the ward Fran was on; he slowed down as he approached her room, as though if he delayed the terrible news for as long as he could, it might never happen. Then he saw Jane sitting there; she saw him and got up out of her chair; she met him at the door. To Andy's surprise, she embraced him, tears were rolling down her cheeks. She did not speak for many moments, neither could Andy. Eventually he did speak.

"Is she gone?" Jane dried her eyes with her sleeve.

"Where were you?"

"I came as soon as I could. I am so sorry. When did it happen?" Andy said.

"They said there were no signs. They were going to switch the machine off."

"Did they?" he asked. Jane looked at him directly in his eyes.

"Just when they were about to, something happened; something of a miracle. Her signs started coming back."

"She is alive?"

"Yes." Jane said, nodding. Andy entered the room. There was a doctor and a nurse by Fran's bedside.

"You are Francesca's father?" The doctor asked.

"Yes. How is she?"

"Her illness has gone into remission. As swiftly as it came, it seems to have gone. We do need to do more tests, but thankfully she is rapidly improving."

Andy looked down at his daughter's small frame. She seemed too innocent to have been caught up in all of this mess. He caught sight of John standing just outside the door and he asked Jane to excuse him for a moment whilst he spoke with him. They looked at each other with relief and gratitude.

"Was this you somehow?" Andy asked John.

"I got the gift back...it came back to me."

"Thank you."

"What happened in India?"

"It's a long story, but I did get it back. When I thought I was too late to save Fran, I passed it onto Dominic, though not in the way that he wanted. He more or less kidnapped me."

"Seriously, he went to those lengths? He had been pushing me for information. The guy's insane. He has the gift now?"

"Not really. He locked me in a building, that's why I was so late getting here. I'll tell you the whole story later. Thanks again John."

"I'll leave you to it. Call me if you need anything." John said, before turning around and leaving. Andy went back over to Fran and looked across at Jane.

"Is Jack ok?" he asked.

"He's fine. He's with my mum."

Andy was about to touch Fran on the forehead; he didn't do it: wary of just what might happen. He wondered about this *gift* that had existed for thousands of years. Had anyone else ever had so many ups and downs with it? Now a sense of overwhelming relief hit him and with it came the physical exhaustion that his mind had been hiding from him.

"You look shattered." Jane told him.

"You don't look too good yourself." Andy replied.

"Go and get some sleep."

"Ok. I will, but when I come back later, you

can go and get some yourself."

"Deal. This chair is comfier than it looks, but not *that* comfy. I haven't slept much for days." Jane said, "Go on then, come back in a few hours. Then maybe you can tell me why you were in India."

Andy took her advice and left the hospital. John was just pulling off the car park when he saw Andy coming out of the main entrance; he stopped and offered him a lift. In another car on the car park, Sean and Gary also spotted Andy leaving, they followed behind John's car.

"You look worn out." John said to Andy as he was driving.

"I feel it. I'm just gonna grab a few hours sleep, if you could drop me off at home."

"So what happened…the brief version?"

"I found the guy in India, or rather he found me and, this *is* the short version, I got the gift back, eventually."

"What was he like?"

"Amazing guy. He's kept the gift  more or less his whole life, like Peter said. He's in his eighties, I think, but looks a lot younger. Anyway, Dominic wanted the power to heal for himself and he got it. Though not the version he wanted."

"The guy is actually borderline psychotic."

"I don't think he's borderline, he *is* psychotic." Andy said, "I'll tell you the full story in the next couple of days. I am just so grateful you helped

Fran."

"According to Peter, when you lost the gift, it came back to its previous host...myself. It makes sense if you think about it."

"Hey, none of this makes sense to me. You know, come to think of it, Ramesh said the same thing happened with him. The power to heal returned to him after it went wrong when *he* had passed it on to someone else. I didn't know that could happen until he told me. I am just so glad it's over."

"So Dominic received a different version of the gift?"

"I passed it to Dominic, but he seemed to take on the afflictions of the people he healed. I didn't wish for that to happen, it just did."

"It has to be for the right reasons, otherwise it won't work properly. Also, with me and you both having the gift at the same time, perhaps it caused a glitch, perhaps something went wrong. Maybe I will go and see him tomorrow; I might be able to fix him. Though some would say he doesn't deserve it."

"I no longer see any auras. Perhaps I am back to how I was before all this." Andy said, flatly.

"I see a paler version of the golden haze above you once again. I think you *are* back to how you were."

"Great. I did want off that rollercoaster."

They arrived at Andy's flat and he got out, still

holding the bag of money, "Look, I want to give you some of this; it's a pay-off from Dom for the gift, I didn't really *earn* it. Get a bigger boat." Andy gestured towards the cash.

"You keep it...or give it back. Dominic already gave some to me when he was desperate for information. It's not like he needs it back."

"Are you sure? I will keep hold of it for now. I suppose I did keep up my end of the bargain, though the result was not what he wanted. By the way, I'm not going back to the Haven. I've quit."

"Understandable. Keep in touch." John said, before driving off. Andy walked up the path to his flat. Then he heard a voice behind him and, turning around, he saw Sean and Gary standing there. He ran to the door, but moving surprisingly fast for two big men, they got to him before he turned the key in the door.

"Dominic wants a quiet word." Sean said.

"No chance" Andy said. Gary gripped him; Andy span around and threw a punch to Gary's jaw that caused him to stagger back momentarily. Sean smiled in approval. The next thing Andy felt was a whack on the back of his head, and then everything went black.

◆ ◆ ◆

When Andy regained consciousness and his eyes adjusted to his surroundings, he recognised the faith healing room at the Haven, just moments before he heard Dom's voice.

"You did it wrong. Do it again." Andy sat up on the table in the middle of the room. They must have placed him on there whilst he was out cold.

"I can't, I mean, I don't have it. You have it."

"I haven't got *it*. It's no good to me like this; do you think it's funny that I have taken on the symptoms of the patients? Look at me."

"I did not intend that. Something went wrong." Andy said.

"You're not kidding. Now you're going to put it right, *then* you can quit." Dom rasped. *Should Andy have told Dom about John?...No.* This guy was out of control, he had just had him accosted and kidnapped for a second time. The back of his head was throbbing with pain and there was blood on his hand where he had felt it. Dom wheeled himself over to Andy and held out his hand. "Try again." Andy realised that his options were limited. He held out his hand to clasp Dom's, once again, then slowly brought his other hand on top of that one to form the circuit needed. He did not know what to expect, he was not sure what, if any, power he had retained, though he did feel that *something* would happen. They remained in this position for a few seconds, and then they both felt a tingling sensation that built up to a minor electric shock. Then, at the exact moment that feeling subsided, the candles in the room blew out as though from a sudden ghostly gust of air. Something *different* had happened. Andy slowly let go of Dom's hand and they both waited, each of them knew that *something* was different. *Have the intention to heal*. Before long, a smile flickered across Dom's face. The painful sensation in his joints was subsiding. He breathed more easily and stood upright. It had worked. He walked over to the bag with the money in it that he had previously given to Andy.

"I'll take this back." he said. He looked at Andy in a hateful way that made Andy concerned about what his own fate would be. Sean and Gary stood between him and the door; they had witnessed the strange events and awaited Dom's next instructions, "So now, what do we do with you?" Dom said, with the sardonic smile firmly back in place. He would have to punish this cook for the audacity he had shown, and he had already made up his mind. Then, as he placed the bag of money down again, he noticed a cut on his hand. No big deal. Then a moment later, he spotted blood coming from a gash on his thumb. *Was there something sharp on the bag?* Then he coughed up a lump of phlegm...then a second one. A moment later and he had a searing pain in his head. Sean and Gary looked at each other in bewilderment. Andy suddenly realised what was happening to Dom: he was manifesting the symptoms of *everyone* that he himself had ever healed...*dozens* of people. Before long, Dom was on the floor. No one person could survive that many afflictions all at once, his body just couldn't take it. Sean went over to Dom when he'd stopped moving and placed his hand on his neck.

"He's dead." Sean said, calmly.

"What happened?" Gary asked. Sean shrugged as he looked at Andy, not really having the first clue of what was going on; it was well beyond his comprehension and pay scale, "What do we do?"

"I don't know what's just happened. I don't want to know...whatever it is." Sean said. He turned to Andy, "Do we need to shut you up?" Andy shook his head; he looked convincing enough for Sean to believe him. Perhaps he would have *shut him up* anyway, but even he was struggling to take in what he'd just seen in front of him.

"Here, take the money. I don't want it." Andy said. He thought that this gesture might smooth over things with Sean and Gary. Sean took the bag and looked under the towel covering the wads of notes. He didn't say anything, but zipped it back up; happy enough to come out ahead with this cash windfall.

"I'll tell them he's gotten worse." Sean said, "Lets go, you duck down in the back of the car, we'll drop you somewhere." he said to Andy. The three calmly left out of the side door. Sean went back inside the building to tell Penny the news that Dom seemed to have gotten worse during their *meeting*, but did not let on that he knew the full extent of Dom's condition. When Penny went down to check on him, she found him in the wheelchair, a strange colour and not breathing. She called the doctor again, but this time she knew it was too late.

Sean and Gary drove through the grounds of the Haven in silence with Andy in the back. They stopped on a remote stretch of road where they knew there was no CCTV. Sean realised he would probably be called back for questions later, but for now he just wanted to get away with the money. As far as anyone else knew, he thought Dom was still alive when he left. Sean spoke as Andy got out.

"I don't know what happened back there, but I don't have to tell you to keep your mouth shut do I?"

"No. I won't say anything." replied Andy.

"Not like *we* did anything anyway." Sean added before driving off. Andy checked his pocket; his hand felt one of the wads of notes in there that he had managed to get out of the bag. He didn't check it at the time, but when safely back in his flat, he saw that it was a wad of £10,000 in £50 notes. He placed it in the sock drawer, set his alarm and slept.

◆ ◆ ◆

He relieved Jane later that day. The doctor said that they were bringing Fran out of the induced coma later and Jane went home to grab a few hours sleep before that happened. John called Andy as he sat watching over Fran.

"Do you know Dominic is dead?" John asked.

Andy whispered back. "I was hit over the head and taken to him again. Just after you dropped me off. He thought I had deliberately messed him up."

"Hadn't you?"

"...Anyway, he insisted on me trying to fix him. He grabbed my hand. It was very strange."

"What happened?"

"Well it did fix him, briefly. Then, he seemed to take on the symptoms of *everyone* I had ever healed. It was even weirder than anything else I have seen and that's saying something. But I am worried that if I touch anyone else, there might be a problem. What do you think?"

"I think you will be fine. Somehow, I *know* you will be fine. The story at the Haven is that he died of natural causes. Of course there will be a post-mortem."

"I suppose that *is* true...a *lot* of them. Good luck to whoever carries that out. What are you going to do?" Andy asked.

Well, the big consortium takeover is off, or so they are saying. I think Felicity might take over at the Haven; that's what one or two are saying, and it is hers now after all."

"Are you going to carry on there?"

"Yeah, I'll carry on a bit longer. See what happens. You don't want me to pass the gift back on to you then?"

"I'll pass on that one. I think it's better suited to you."

"Are you still quitting, now that Dom has... gone?"

"Yeah, not only that, I'm done with catering. I'm going to find something else to do. Anyway, keep in touch and John, thanks once again." He ended the call as Jane entered the room, along with Jack and the doctor. Andy smiled and hugged Jack. Before long, Fran was fully conscious and sitting up in bed.

"Have I been asleep for a long time dad?" she asked.

"For a while." Andy replied.

"I had a long dream."

"What about Fran?" Andy asked.

"We were feeding the ducks and it was raining. Can we feed the ducks this week please?"

"Yes, yes we can."

# ABOUT THE AUTHOR

## Peter Birkett

Peter likes to let his imagination off the leash and he delves into the realm of fantasy and the unkown. What is lurking just under the surface of everyday life? Some of his characters are inspired by people that you might walk past in the street and he believes that truth is often as strange as fiction. Whilst still at school, the dad of two once got sent to the headmaster's office. Fearing the worst, he was relieved to see the much feared headmaster holding his English creative writing book. He wasn't in trouble, the headmaster wanted to him to do something with his talent...years later he started on a journey to fulfill the headmaster's wish.

# BOOKS BY THIS AUTHOR

## Midas

Sometimes in life, average people can become extraordinary and that's what happened to small town thirtysomething Andy gold. The power to heal others, it couldn't be real...or could it? Heal someone once per day from dusk till dawn, but don't be selfish with it, or things might go horribly wrong...

## Chiller

After the crazy events of the last few months, Andy Gold was settling back into normal life. Things were looking up, or so it seemed, until digging at a construction site on the edge of town unearthed something. People started to go missing.
Events that were set in motion in the dim and distant past were about to come to an

Earth-chilling climax. Something ancient and malevolent had returned and the world would never be the same. What were these strange gemstoned rings that had been passed down from generation to generation?
By fate or by chance or just plain bad luck, Andy once again found himself positioned right in the eye of the storm.

## Viral

One last threat. That was how Ramesh the psychic had described it to Andy Gold. One last mission and then it would be a long run of peace and normality. It sounded straight forward enough, all that he needed to do was embark on a long journey and then kill an evil other worldly assassin in order to stop a deadly pandemic from wiping out the human race...what could go wrong?

Printed in Great Britain
by Amazon

10905859R00192